THE TESSERACT CODEX
DARK STAR

A Science Fiction

Novel

By WP Parker

Published in the United States by:

Five Moons Publications
155 Carol Lane
Elma, NY 14059-9749
www.fivemoons.org
fivemoonscifi@outlook.com

Disclaimer: This is a work of fiction. Names, characters, businesses, organizations, places, events, and incidents are the product of the author's imagination and as such are used fictitiously. Any resemblance to actual persons, living or dead, businesses, organizations, events, or locales is entirely coincidental, except for Elm Cove. It really did exist in this time stream. All of the stories, characters, places, events, and things presented in this novel are the intellectual property of William P. Parker.

Please visit my website. Sign up for my newsletter for upcoming book releases, free books, and free audiobook promo codes.

www.fivemoons.org

Prologue

Clay of Earth, know this to the very core of you: yours were the people cast into the outer darkness because of the evil in their hearts.

A gift was made to them of Tesseract, but they were found unworthy.

Clay of Earth, you do not see how entangled in each other's fates you are. Each life is entangled in all of the others, and now mine is entangled with yours.

Clay of Earth, Leaf in the Wind, you are of them but not like them. We found you full of darkness from your trials at the hands of the most evil, yet in your despair, you became the empty vessel. Into that empty vessel, we poured the light of truth. And so you found beauty in the light of four moons. My soul sings songs of joy in that. You are welcome. And so the next step together we must take. The Tesseract Codex is the key to knowledge. You must do more than just to know it. You must become it.

Leaf in the wind, the gift that once was made to the unworthy, was only the first step. Beyond the Tesseract is all that really matters.

-- The one who stands in the Tesseract's shadow --

CHAPTER ONE
In the beginning.

In the beginning, there was peace, and John Korbin was a leaf in the wind. Life was good. That all seemed like a million years ago now. Then war came. The Syndicate's mercenaries waged a war on the Union like no other, tearing lives asunder, destroying everything in their path, leaving only sadness and chaos in their wake. The mercenary forces under Sarsen Tabbot leveled John's home world. They killed his wife and daughter. They killed his whole family. They burned his whole homeworld to the ground. And that changed everything.

At first, John was full of pain and anger. That turned into rage, and John took his pound of flesh, but in the end, that left him empty, and sad, and alone. It left a big hole in his heart. Once more, John became the leaf in the wind. He filled that gaping empty hole inside of him with silence. Every day he had to force himself to put one foot in front of the other. He buried himself in his studies so that he wouldn't have time to remember. He refused to allow himself one second of self-pity. Instead, he turned that driving force to earn a degree in starship engineering and he went to Union Fleet's own War College, determined to learn whatever it took to inflict revenge.

Then came the end of the war and once more that changed everything. Union Fleet no longer needed the millions of veterans that now suddenly found themselves alone on the outside, embroiled in the chaos that ensued. His past once more swept away, John had no choice but to start over. So, he went to the Union Fleet space docks with all good intentions. He intended to start his life over. He intended to buy a war surplus scout-class ship.

Instead, he unknowingly bought the Tesseract.

In the beginning, John walked onto the decks of the Tesseract, and that changed everything. But John was still empty, and sad, and alone. Jessica, his oversexed but highly talented artificial copilot, changed that. Jane, the ship's motherly android cook, changed that. His good buddy Hack, the maintenance android with an attitude, changed that. And most of all, his beloved Mariah, tough little cookie to the very artificial core of her, changed that. Even the ship itself changed. It once more wore its name proudly -- the Tesseract.

And all of that was fine until he discovered that Mariah Jane Harrington, Jessica Ann Miller, Jane Marie Schultz, and Henry James Merritt were all listed as the crew of a starship like no other, a starship made with alien timequake technology. They were not listed as artificials on that ship at all but as humans, lost in the line of duty. Once more, knowing that changed everything.

That set his mind on fire to uncover the truth. After all, the truth shall set you free -- right? Isn't that what they tell you? Well, they couldn't have been more wrong! He got the truth alright. Special Forces Admiral Johnson eventually gave him the files. Now, there was a full dose of the truth if he had ever seen one.

John read the Special Forces report of the rescue mission by Captain Michael Jacobi, in total disbelief and disgust. It said that when the rescue craft arrived at the site of the time-space disaster, the ship was so distorted that it was no longer recognizable as a frigate class starship, but there was an anoza ship alongside. Captain Jacobi was not at all upset to find that none of the human crew had survived. Oh, really? He was, however, very upset when he found out that the anoza had moved their essence into the artificial intelligence processors on board the Tesseract just before they died. Now there you go!

Then the anoza summarily informed Jacobi that they intended to 'restore' the crew, but he would not hear of that. Oh no! Of course not! Jacobi could not allow the anoza to restore what may have been the only witnesses to what had actually happened. Oh, no. He couldn't have any witnesses to expose the evil that was done purely as the result of human greed and arrogance. Oh, no. He sure couldn't have that.

Instead, Captain Jacobi insisted that all of the artificial intelligence processors be shut down. The anoza were outraged, and rightly so! They called him a murderer! They were upset that the humans were about to kill four of their own, stubbornly refusing to listen to them, but what was new about that? The arrogant, self-righteous humans hadn't listened to anything that the anoza had told them. So, why should this be any different? Jacobi quoted some stupid human laws about desecrating the deceased, but by that point, the anoza had heard enough. They left, never to be seen again.

Ever since he read that file, John was determined that Jacobi's report would not be the final word. He sat quietly in the mess of the Tesseract eating some of Jane's finest homemade pickles thinking about all of this, calm on the outside. Normally, all of this ran down the back roads of his mind like a distant rumble of thunder, but sometimes, when he least expected, that storm unleashed its fury on him. He took in a deep breath and exhaled the vile rage that storm had dredged up.

I am a leaf in the wind, John thought to himself. Another deep breath returned his mind once more to calm. As John finished his pickles, he chose instead to remember the Tesseract's first mission to rescue Emma from the mercenaries and Sophie from the growls. That changed everything too.

~~~

Across the sector from John, on a world far away, mercenary Sub-Commander Rhianna remembered that mission too but from a totally different point of view. She remembered that it had all started with a running gunfight. Somehow, the Union scum had found the base, and that changed everything. That was the beginning of the end. That forced Santo to move the timetable for his invasion of Panara-5 up to right away. It forced Santo to move his mercenary battle group quickly forward or lose the element of surprise. Santo could no longer wait to develop a line of support. He had to leave this small group of people to that task alone. Santo left Rhianna in charge here because that was her specialty – materiel
~~~

support.

And what brought on that running gunfight? A small group of greedy bastards trying to make a pile of gold for hanging on to some little girl named Emma. And what good did that do them? None! That's how much good it did them. For all of their sneaking and conniving, the damned locals stole all their gold right out from under them! Well, there you go! If that wasn't bad enough, Santo pitched a fit when he found out and had the lot of them executed. So, there you go! At least Santo got the base fixed back up and secure before he left. He even left Rhianna with two orbital transports, for whatever good they would do her now.

"I think back to the day that we watched them leave," Rhianna spoke her thoughts out loud to Lucia. "There was no thought of them not coming back. 'See you soon,' they said when they left to take Panara-5 from the Union. How long ago was that? A year… maybe more?"

"Almost two," Lucia corrected her. "But even worse, they went quiet on the com."

"Quiet? Hell! They disappeared altogether." Rhianna voiced her anger and worst fear. "They abandoned us here! They left us here to rot… forever, without hope."

"Stop that! There is always hope. We just have to survive; that's all," Lucia argued.

"Well, there you go. You hit that nail squarely on the head. That's all we are left with now – to live out our days here trying to survive."

"Ishmael hasn't given up hope. Every day he tries something new," Lucia told her.

"More like he is trying my patience. The man isn't good for much," Rhianna continued to complain.

"What do you mean, 'isn't good for much?' He works hard at whatever tasks you give him," Lucia reminded Rhianna. She was tired of Rhianna's incessant bitching and complaining. Besides, Lucia liked Ishmael. He was not your typical arrogant, aggressive Merc man. He was a quiet and soft-spoken man with a gentle face, despite his size. His excellent physical condition was the result of necessity. It came from being forced to defend himself from the likes of the more aggressive Merc men. In fact, Ishmael had quite a reputation from those who had tried, and failed, to beat him. Even so, it's not something you would ever hear from him. He was as modest as he was gentle.

~~~

Kiroc was not at all like Ishmael. He was the typical aggressive, assertive Merc man, but he was not big, nor strong, nor a good fighter, like Ishmael. Kiroc also had a vile temper at times. Today, Kiroc was just plain angry at every damned thing, so he was out hunting. Kiroc hunted growls. He hated them. Kiroc had a long list of everything that he hated, but for now, he could hate the growls.

These growls were nasty beasts without a doubt, like mountain lions on steroids. As if one of them alone was not bad enough, they hunted in packs. A pack of hungry growls could rip a man to shreds in minutes, so Kiroc hunted them in a pulse-cannon walker. That was a lot safer than hunting them on foot. The walker was made from alloys and carbon fiber materials tough enough to survive on a battlefield, so even the most ferocious pack of hungry growls was no match for it.

Ferocious was a good description of growls. The beasts were almost unbelievably ferocious. If you killed one and left the carcass, the others would find it and devour it or fight over it amongst themselves. These things were so bad that prides of them lived openly on the grassy plains near the edge of the forest. Sometimes, they hunted prey in the forest, but most of them could be found on the grassy plains where grazing animals could easily be found for a handy snack.

Because he hated these things so, Kiroc had hunted them to extinction for a 100km radius around base camp over the past year or so. The problem was, when you live in growl territory, clearing an area only created a vacuum for more growls to fill… And so they did. In the meantime, in the absence of the growls, everything else flourished. That made it an even more attractive vacuum for other growls to fill.

While that had worked in Kiroc's favor in the past, lately he wasn't doing so well. He had recently begun to venture beyond his 100km hunt
~~~

zone to find what few of them were left. Rhianna wasn't happy at all when he was gone hunting for days on end, sometimes for weeks on end, but quite frankly, he didn't give a rat's ass anymore what Rhianna thought. He had two weeks' food and water. He told her where he was going and the walker had combat com, so frak her if she didn't like it. Hunting was his only outlet.

The pulse cannon walker was like wearing an exoskeleton. In it, he could walk or run, and jump. It could crouch down low to hide. It could move very fast or silently very slow. It made Kiroc the big man that he was not. In his mind, it made him the invincible fighter. Kiroc moved on farther out, to a valley he could see in the distance. If there were any growls left, that would be where he would find them.

~~~

Ishmael worked all morning on the task list that Rhianna had given him. He was the most technically competent one of the group, so his main task was to keep this whole place running. Every morning, his first task was to check all of the fusion reactors to be sure they were fine and had plenty of fuel. He never told Rhianna that the reactors would run just fine for a hundred years without him ever checking them at all. He never mentioned that the fuel already in them would last even longer. He never told her that the maintenance androids already knew exactly how to fix any faults, either. Instead, he used that time for his own purposes. It was his quiet, peaceful time, free from Rhianna's constant bitching and complaining at him.

Ishmael wandered behind the buildings into one of the orbital transports. He quickly found its quantum-com. Sure; Rhianna had already tried that. Sure, all she got was bad news, but then it got worse. After a while, no one even bothered to answer her calls anymore. That was the pits of despair. Oh, they were out there all right, but the few that were left had abandoned them to their fate. That's when Rhianna gave up hope for a rescue and became very bitter.

Ishmael refused to give up, but he needed a plan. He sure did not lack for time to think, so that is what he did. He gladly took on all of those
~~~

useless tasks that Rhianna insisted on listing for him every day. While he went through the motions of those tasks, he was deep in thought. If the Merc forces were as scattered as what he had heard over the com when there was traffic, then there had to be some of them scattered this way, or so he reasoned.

Today he would start looking for them. He just needed to be persistent and not give up. Despite his lack of formal training, Ishmael was quick to learn whatever he needed to. So, for hours he sat, studying the built-in manuals, working the quantum-com, trying to make contact. He learned to program alerts to his personal network node for all of the popular meeting nodes on the Merc network.

Chapter Two

It doesn't get stranger than this.

Mariah could no longer contain her overwhelming curiosity, and Jessica was every bit as curious as Mariah. Jessica watched as John headed for the galley, intent on stealing another sample of those damned good bread-and-butter pickles again.

"He's gone to the galley again," Jessica whispered to her cohort in crime.

"Come on," Mariah led her fellow sneak and snoop off to recon John's office.

The door to his office opened for them as they approached. They closely examined his 3D display. It was covered with equations and strange symbols.

"What is that?" Jessica asked Mariah in a low whisper.

"It looks like a list of equations," Mariah stated the obvious.

"What are we looking for?" John asked in a normal voice from behind them.

"Oh, I was just curious," Mariah told him with her best innocent look.

"I am with her." Jessica didn't even bother to mount a defense.

"It is exactly what it appears to be," he told them. "It is a step-by-step list of the eleven-dimensional equations necessary to very precisely set the engine fields for a timequake jump."

Mariah looked at it for a few seconds before she decided, "It looks just like a program."

"Hm. I hadn't thought about it like that, but yes, I guess it does, doesn't it? Sometimes good ideas just happen, and you just sparked one. Could you make this into a nav program for me?"

"Yes, I guess I could," Mariah admitted, but now she was upset with herself. Her damned snooping just got her more work. That got the ball rolling. As it turned out, John had already done the hard part by listing all of those 119 eleven-dimensional equations in proper sequence. Linking in all of the required sensor measurements and the interstellar database was a simple task for Mariah.

In only a few hours, the program was ready to try. Mariah ran the current nav setup of two separate computers first for 100 test jumps, and she wasn't making them easy ones either. The test jumps would all be through the worst convoluted space that that she could make them. She pulled up all of the data from their dense space jumps through the Devil's Pitchfork and put those in there too. The current nav setup spit out one answer every seventeen seconds, so she had to let that run for a half-hour to get all the answers she needed.

Then she set up the test on a single nav computer with the new program and hit the button. The answers all appeared in what seemed like an instant.

"Holy crap! That was fast!" John was duly impressed. "How long did it actually take?"

"It took… 113.7 microseconds," Mariah read the answer, much to her own surprise as well.

"Let me see. Let me see," John wanted to see the results. "Wow… And those answers are derived directly from the equations. There are no approximations anywhere in those answers at all. Okay. I now have a perfect solution for my eleven-dimensional nav for the Tesseract! Let's go make it happen on all the rest of our ships!"

"Hey! Hey! Wait one minute here!" Mariah slowed him down. "This program will only work on the Tesseract. All of the other ships need the equations for the four-dimensional tetrahedron engine configuration." She thought for sure that would slow him down.

"Right here," John showed her. He already had all of those equations in yet another file. She looked at them, now really pissed off that her snooping only made more work for her.

"I really wish you could find us another job," Mariah complained. "You might like doing all of this technical work on your damned starships, but I am getting sick and damned tired of it. I would much rather be blowing up somebody's hoosegow."

"Yeah, blowing up a hoosegow sounds like a lot more fun to me, too," Jessica agreed.

"Okay," he assured them. "After we get all this work done, we will find us a real job."

"Yeah, yeah, yeah. That's what you always say," Mariah continued to complain.

"When you need a break," John offered, "we can go to the Pig and Whistle. I'll order a Reuben." There was some mystical connection with John and Reubens and 'jobs.' Whenever he ordered one, the whole staff at the Pig and Whistle went on Red Alert.

~

Two days later, John checked over the task list for his four captured mercenary M-4 fighters acquired in their last 'job.' His top work items were to hide the copilot's artificial intelligence processors under the floor plates and to get the nav computers reprogrammed. He was caught in one of those personal conundrums that happen every now and then. While he was quick to extend his love to Kira and Gina, his two lovely Merc houseguests, they were simply not family. To John, unless you were family, trust was earned over time. So, while he was modifying the M-4s, he preferred that Kira and Gina didn't know a damned thing about what he was doing.

The problem was that Kira sometimes spent her personal think time in her old M-4 fighter, the one with Lisa as the copilot. To partially solve that problem, John had Hack do all of the physical changes to the M-4s at night while Kira slept. All that was left for daytime work was some programming that could be done while Kira, Sam, and Gina went into town.

They were going back to a place called 'Taffy's' that John and Mariah had just recently discovered. Taffy's had been in business on Panara-5 for 147 years. They had real throwback food for sure – hot dogs and hamburgers cooked on a charcoal grill and curly french-fries cooked in hot vegetable oil. There were outdoor seats and little birds everywhere. Taffy's had a sign that read, 'Today I am as happy as a bird with a french-fry.' The little brown birds were terrible beggars, but everyone fed them. Everyone who tried the place loved it. John's favorite was the 'foot long hot dogs.' Loaded up with condiments, they were a real treat but very messy.

~

The next day, Kira went out to her old M-4. She just wanted to sit alone in it and think. Instead, she found John in it working on something.

"Hi, what are you doing?" she asked out of curiosity.

"I am hooking up the original Merc com module," he told her. This was not a secret. "I couldn't put it on the network, so I hooked it up to its own display." John turned it on. It cycled through a number of startup screens before it began monitoring the Merc com traffic. A slowly growing list appeared. The list grew in bursts. It was working.

"What's wrong?" John asked when he saw the look on her face. "Are you homesick?"

"I don't know. For some reason, I still feel so totally lost and disoriented."

"After the war, I felt lost and alone. It was like my heart had been ripped out," John told her. "I lost my wife and daughter to Sarsen's Expeditionary Forces. Sarsen killed my whole family. She left nothing of my home world but scorched earth. Even so, for some strange reason even I don't know, I still wanted to return home after the war. I felt like, if I had to start over, I would start over from there. Then I found the Tesseract, and that changed everything."

"Mercs killed your whole family, and you don't hate us all?"

"No. You didn't kill my family. Sarsen did," he told her straight out. "I don't hate Mercs. I do hate Sarsen. It took me a long time to be able to say that. I had to figure it out for myself first, but I did."

Kira hugged him and put her head on his chest. "In all of this huge galaxy, I don't feel so alone anymore."

"I just told you all about me, but I still don't even know your whole name."

"I am Kirabatti Tobruk," she told him with a smile.

"Oh? Like the famous navigator and explorer, Ishmael Tobruk?"

"He is my ancestor," she answered John proudly.

"Really? I read Ishmael Tobruk's navigational notes all the time. The man was brilliant."

"He would have been so happy to hear that. In every generation since him, there has been an Ishmael Tobruk named after him. My father is the seventh son with his name. I haven't had any word from my father or mother in a very long time. I miss them so much."

"Well then, maybe you can help us both," he told her. "I had this idea that there might be a lot of Mercs out there in exactly the same predicament that you were in after the war. That is why I am hooking up this Merc quantum com unit. Maybe we can find them."

"I will try," she told him.

~

John found Kira two days later in the M-4, crying.

"What's wrong?" he asked.

"I found my Father!" she told him, but her tears did not look like tears of joy to him.

"But there is something wrong?" he surmised.

"He is stranded on some far outworld," she told him.

"I seem to have an awful lot of starships here. I think we can solve that problem," he told her, but more was wrong. He could tell. "And?"

"He fears that my mother was killed or lost."

"What battle group was she with?"

"Santo's," Kira told him.

"That may actually be good news. Most of Santo's people were taken prisoner after the battle of Panara-5. Come on. Let's go see if Mariah can help us with that." Now that stopped the tears. They found Mariah relaxing in the mess with her tea and some of her fancy, pilgrim cookies.

"If you are looking for me to do any more work on your damned starships, you can just go pound salt in your ass," she threatened him without ever looking up from her tea. It was a new old Earth saying that she had just picked up and was waiting for a chance to hit him with it.

"Oh, no," John told her. "It's not for me. It's for Kira."

Mariah looked up with a smile. "Oh, well, that's a different story. What do you need my help with, dear?" she asked Kira.

Kira explained the situation to her as they made their way to Mariah's workstation on the bridge. "Well, the Captain was right. There were a number of Merc groups. Some were still determined to make a go of it while others just want it all to end. One group led me to another. Suddenly, this morning, I was face-to-face with my father! That was wonderful, but then he told me of my mother's fate."

"What is your mother's name?" Mariah asked her.

"Nomi Setranno," Kira told Mariah. "She is like you, a Science Officer."

Mariah got into the Union Fleet database. "Yes, she is… and… She still is. She is in a settlement right here on Panara-5. The Union had no way to repatriate the Mercs after the battle, so that was the best that they could do for now."

"My mother is here? On Panara-5? Can we go get her?!"

"Of course, we can," Mariah told her. Then she looked at John.

"I'll get the LZ ready," he told them. Word quickly spread throughout the ship, turning this into everybody was going. Mariah got the Fleet paperwork all signed to get Nomi released into their care while everybody else got ready. Kira was amazed at the support she was getting for this, as the LZ full of people lifted into the traffic for a suborbital hop to the settlement.

A weary-looking, middle-aged woman got off the Fleet ground transport and came walking into the Union Fleet Administration building with her duffle bag, not knowing at all what to expect. She was certainly not expecting to find a whole crowd of people there and never would have suspected for one minute that they were there for her.

"Kira!" she cried when they spotted each other. Nomi dropped her bag and ran to her daughter. Everyone gave them some time just to hold each other, and cry and hug.

"I found Dad!" Kira told her mother. Nomi looked around.

"No, he is not here. He is stranded on a far outworld, but we are going to get him."

"We?" Nomi asked. That started a whole round of introductions, for which no one expected Nomi to actually remember anybody's names just yet.

It was about then that the Union Fleet people suggested that this reunion be moved to somewhere else. It was their kind invitation to leave, and so they did. Kira spent the whole trip home bringing Nomi up to the present and explaining how she came to be on the Tesseract.

Their arrival back home was a bit confusing at first, but Kira and Nomi made a side trip to Lisa's M-4 to call Kira's father. Everyone gave them their privacy, but Lisa overheard every word. Needless to say, Lisa told Jessica. Jessica told Mariah. That is just how their 'social network' worked. John just rolled his eyes in disbelief.

Mariah put her hands on her hips and told him, "Women communicate better than men."

"And way more frequently," he couldn't resist the chance to jab her.

"Pow! Zoom!" she threatened him with a clenched fist, but he was laughing.

"Hm," John considered, "this is not exactly what I would have called a job."

"Well, you did have a Reuben at the Pig and Whistle," Jessica remembered. "We thought that nothing happened, but maybe it just took its own sweet time to work."

"Okay. I am good with that. So, I am going to call this a job," Mariah decided. "It is a job if I am not the one assigned to do all of the work. We have to go rescue Kira's father from some far outworld. That ranks as a job in my book, and it is way better than you dreaming up more damned programming work for me to do on your damned starships and driving me absolutely bat shits."

"That's a short drive," John commented under his breath.

"We have a job?" Jessica asked just to be sure. "Great! Do I get to blow something up this time?"

"No. This is just a simple rescue of a stranded father," John told her… or so he thought.

Kira and Nomi walked back over to the Tesseract and into the mess. It had become the natural gathering place for everyone. Jane brought out the snacks, and everyone just relaxed and had a nice chat.

"Did you get the coordinates of that world where your father is?" John asked Kira.

"Yes, I did. I put them on this tablet." She handed it to Jessica. Jessica's smile suddenly turned flat. She gave Mariah a funny look.

[Dear Lord! He was one of the mercenaries on Sophie's world! That is where he is stranded. Do you even believe this?] she linked privately over the network.

[Unbelievable… John, did you see this?]

[Good Lord! It doesn't get stranger than this,] he agreed.

[You really do have to stop saying that!] Mariah scolded him. [You thought it didn't get stranger than letting a couple of Merc girls stay with us. Well, it just did!]

[When you're right, you're right,] John had to once more agree. [Now, I'm almost afraid to ask, what's next?]

[And well you should be,] Jessica agreed with Mariah.

"Kira," John told her. "I think I should maybe have a talk with your father before we make way. He needs to understand how this has to be done. Let's go make another call."

John, Kira, and Nomi went out to Lisa's M-4 to make the call. They had to wait for Ishmael, but his face finally appeared.

"Ishmael," John addressed him. "I am John Korbin. Has Nomi explained to you that your own people lied to you about losing the war?"

"Yes," he replied with disappointment on his face.

"We both explained to him how well we were treated," Nomi told John.

"All we want is an end to this war," Ishmael explained to John.

"We just want to settle down and live our lives in peace, like normal people," Nomi agreed.

"What I hope you see is that surrender is the only option that will let you get on with your lives," John told Ishmael. "I need you to convince your compatriots of that too. I can bring you back to Panara-5, but from that point on, your future will be up to you."

Ishmael thought about that for a few seconds. He let out a long sigh.

"I have no problem with surrender. I think Lucia will be fine with that too, but I also know that Kiroc will definitely be a problem. The arrogant little monster is out in one of the pulse-cannon walkers killing those terrible growling beasts just for the sport of it. Rhianna may be a problem and maybe not. I don't know. She was put in charge when Santo left us here. She thinks she still is. All that I can say is that I will do what I can."

"Thank you. This rescue will work if everyone just keeps a calm head," John told Ishmael. "Let me assure you that I do not want anyone killed. The war is over. No one needs to die anymore. As I said, this will work if everyone just keeps a calm head."

~

"We are doing what?" Kip questioned John's sanity after John filled him in.

"Yeah, yeah, I know. Rescuing Mercs is not exactly what I ever thought I would be doing after the war, but it is Kira's father. Did I tell you that he is Ishmael Tobruk the 7th?"

"Yeah, I think you did, but that was lost in the fact that he was maybe one of the guys we fought to get Emma the hell out of there," Kip replied.

"No. You said that. Kira told me that her father is a stellar cartographer like his ancestors before him. He is not a combatant at all. They left him there because he was 'unnecessary' along with another man and two women to hold the base open for their supply ships to use after they took Panara-5. I guess we pretty much crapped all over that too," John concluded.

"Let me get this straight: we kicked their asses and took Emma. Then Luke and Sam pretty much destroyed the place with pulse-cannon walkers.

Then you engineered the defeat of Santo's entire damned battle group, and now we are going back to rescue their survivors?"

"Yep, that pretty much sums it up," John had to admit.

"Well, I sure don't know why your head isn't spinning with all of that. Mine sure is."

"In the end, I am only clear on one point: we are all only human. Most of the mercenary veterans are just as confused and lost as we are. We will just go on killing each other without any rhyme or reason if we leave them out there all armed to the teeth and with no other means to survive but to make trouble for us. The war isn't just over for the Union. It's over for everybody. Lame-ass pilgrims left us with this God-awful mess, but we are smarter than they are. We know what has to be done."

"I thought we were, but now I am beginning to wonder who the crazy one here is."

"That would be me," John went along with him. "Crazy like a fox."

"Hm, you better talk to Luke about joining us for this mission. You are going to need all of the backup you can get on the Tesseract in case there is trouble."

"I will have Sam go over to Rebecca's place and ask him," John agreed.

Chapter Three
The curiouser it gets.

The Tesseract lifted into the night sky. Kip led the group of four captured mercenary M-4 fighters into the sky behind the Tesseract. Anyone but John would think him totally crazy to fly six ships to rescue four people, but John had ulterior motives. It was more of his crazy-like-a-fox thinking, but if you asked Mariah, John was just a big kid.

"Some boys love their dirt toys. John loves his starships," Mariah told Jessica.

Everyone else settled in and headed for bed. John and Jessica settled in on the bridge. John plotted the course to WXR3341-5. It was three days' journey for him to shake out his new squad of captured mercenary M-4 fighters. It was three days' journey to get his head back into those anoza Codex files. As obsessed as he had been after his family was killed, he now intended to consume those Codex files.

To Jessica, it was three days to spend with her new network of female copilots, teaching them to fly like seasoned fighter pilots, but right now, she was more just teaching them to fly in formation, with fields interlocked, through each jump. To Jessica, flying a starship was like a fine ballet dance. Even the smallest detail of it was important to her.

"How are the copilots doing?" John asked Jessica after a few hours.

"Very good. Lisa catches right on to whatever I show her. Ann and Ciara are doing pretty well too, but Barbie always seems to need help. Is it possible for an artificial woman to be a ditz?"

"Geez, I wouldn't think so, but what do I know about artificial intelligence?" he admitted.

"Huh? You live with artificials all around you," she reminded him of the obvious.

"Yeah, that's the scary part," he teased her.

She gave him a squinty-eyed look in mock protest.

"No, really. I mean it. I thought I knew all about living with artificials. Who hasn't grown up with artificials all around? But then I came aboard the Tesseract and all of that changed." It sure did, but he kept the reason to himself for fear of the emotional damage it could inflict on those he now loved.

"For the better, I hope?" Jessica ventured to ask.

John smiled. "I love you all like family. It couldn't get better than that."

That made Jessica smile. She had her own thoughts on how it could get better.

John stayed up late, enjoying being back into deep space. After everyone else had long since gone to bed, Jessica decided to get into something more comfortable, but you know Jessica. To her, that was just her undies. All that John needed was to see was her naked backside with those anoza tattoos running down her back. That popped the Codex main screen right up on his pilot's display.

[Hey! What's up with that?] Jessica noticed right away.

Oh, Drat! [Your tattoo is the sequence of symbols that open the page,] John explained, but now Jessica had a great big smile on her face.

Oh, yeah, she thought. *Now I know what he sees in his mind to get that screen to pop up*. She went back to work, but the cat was out of the bag. She couldn't stop smiling.

Oh well, John thought, *I may as well do some reading*. And so, he did. He read the next Codex file beyond the tesseract. Hell, what he was reading was beyond the looking glass as far as he was concerned, but such is always the case with quantum physics. It was all about the eleven-dimensional nature of space and matter and the quantum nature of time.

In their typical one-two-three manner, the anoza laid it all out in simple, easy-to-understand blocks. This was way beyond anything he had ever learned in college about time-space, but the anoza were a much older species than humans. They also approached the problem from a totally different perspective. John had to admit, their simple, logical, one block at a time approach taught him in a few hours what four years of lame-ass pilgrim engineering college certainly had not.

The road to hell was paved with good intentions, though. John fell asleep while reading.

Jessica went over and gently nudged him. "Oh, my Captain, you are falling asleep. Get up and go to bed," she whispered to him.

"Hm. That's the best offer I've had all night," he teased her, but she was up for that challenge. She snuggled him good and kissed his ear. That got his attention.

"Okay, bed it is," he finally surrendered, but to her disappointment, it was his own bed.

[Hack,] she called him. [Come to mama. You are in for a rough night tonight.]

~~~

Ishmael was a man of few words but keen intellect. He needed to talk to Lucia. He needed to get her on his side. He needed to do that as quickly as possible now. He found her working alone in the food building. She was putting together a rationing plan so the android cooks would stretch out their available food supply. She figured it would last maybe another year. They would have that long to figure out how to survive off of what this planet had to offer.

As strange as this might sound, the Mercs were much more like pilgrims than outworlders. Their society was so totally focused on war and fighting that outworld survival to them amounted to taking what you needed from the enemy or the local human settlers. Mercs were not very good settlers and even worse outworlders. Rather than sticking together, they often squabbled over resources and who was in charge of what. That was no way to survive in the outworlds at all. It was a surefire road to disaster.

"Lucia, I need to talk to you," Ishmael began slowly. "Santo's battle group was defeated by Union Fleet. The war was lost. Merc forces surrendered to the Union on Zari-Kuut. We need to move on from there."

"What? What do you mean, 'move on?' What the hell are you talking
~~~

about? We are stuck here -- remember? Marooned. Abandoned. Move on? We can't move on."

"We will not be stuck here much longer. There is a ship on the way, a Union ship. They will be here in three days."

"And what then? So, we will be tortured and enslaved?"

"No, not at all. All that our leaders have told us in the past was nothing but a pack of lies to control us and keep us fighting."

"And who told you that? A pack of Union liars?"

"No, not at all. My wife and daughter told me. So, I know that what I am told is the truth."

"I see. So, what do they propose?" Lucia now asked warily.

"Just to lay down our arms and go peacefully. That's all."

"That is all? Oh, really? That is surrender. That is treason."

"Not anymore. The war is over. I never was a warrior, and neither were you. I am sick and tired of living a life of nothing but war. I am done with that whole way of life! All I want to do is to live out my life in peace, like normal people. I think that you do too. Am I right?"

"You are right. I am like you. I never was a warrior. I must admit that it would be nice to live a peaceful life like normal people."

"My hope is to save Rhianna and Kiroc, but that may not happen. I cannot stop them if they are intent on fighting to the last."

"And you think that I can?" Lucia asked him in disbelief.

"No, not at all, but I do want you to know that they will be offered a peaceful way off this planet. They can choose to take it or not. Who knows? They might choose to stand and fight. In that case, the Union forces will do whatever they have to. I don't want to see them die. I would prefer that they choose to live."

"Good luck to you with Kiroc," Lucia warned him. "Who knows? That arrogant little bastard might not even be back from his hunt by the time they get here. He took enough food to last him a couple of weeks."

"Maybe so. He might not get back. In the meantime, how do we go about saving Rhianna from herself?"

"Let me think about it," Lucia told him. "If we wait until the last minute and then subdue her ourselves, at least she would not get herself killed doing something stupid."

"Lucia, I love you dearly as a friend. I hope we are doing the right thing," he told her.

"I hope so, too," Lucia confided in him. "I also consider you a dear friend."

~~~

In the late-night hours, John was barely asleep when a noise outside his room woke him up with a start. He got up and peeked out the door. It was Sophie. In the very dim light, he could just barely see that she was feeling the end of the passageway.

"What are you doing?" John whispered to her.

"There is something here," she whispered back to him, "but I can't seem to open it."

As tired as he was, he stayed up anyway. In the dark, he looked around that passageway. There were four doorways to the staterooms, all closed. Sophie felt around at the very end of the passageway, but she was short. The doors were all automatically operated by sensors high up in the doorjamb. He reached up high and ran his hand along what should have been the top of a doorjamb. In the middle, a sensor picked up his presence. John and Sophie could hear the door open, but they couldn't see it. Sophie trusted her ears and stepped right through what appeared to be a solid wall. John could hardly believe what he just saw but followed her anyway. As they entered the room, the lights all came up automatically. John covered his tired eyes with his hand as their eyes took their own time to adapt.

"If you want to find the special places, then you have to keep trying to find them," Sophie told John.

When John's eyes finally did adjust to the lights, he saw a huge round, black, highly detailed, fabricated ring on its edge at the far end of the room. It was mounted to the floor and the ceiling by some very substantial-looking brackets that also contained the power and control cables.

John walked over close to examine the fine details of the ring. Damn! It looked to him like a huge atomic field generator coil big enough for him to
~~~

walk right through and then some. In fact, there was a ramp on the near side that looked to be for exactly that.

So, where are the controls for this? What does it do? John asked himself.

"We found a new convoluted place," Sophie told him, using Emma's technical word for it.

"Yes, we sure did, but it's very late, and maybe we should be getting back to bed."

"You can go back to bed if you want," Sophie told him. "Maybe I will go sit naked on the bridge with Aunt Jessica and just talk. You know how much Aunt Jessica loves to talk."

John laughed. "Yes, Aunt Jessica sure does love to talk almost as much as you do. Goodnight, my little Sophie." He kissed her goodnight.

"Goodnight, my great big Ka," she told him as she trotted off to the bridge. John crawled back into bed, hoping to finally get some sleep, but Mariah had other ideas. Life was tough for a healthy male on this ship, but somebody had to do it.

~

Morning found John on the short side of sleep, but nonetheless up and about at 07:00. He sat longer than usual in the mess with his java and breakfast. Everyone else would be up at 08:00, so this was his private time. That new convoluted room was a mystery that could not wait. John went up to the bridge, his second cup of java in hand, and pictured Jessica's lovely naked backside in his mind to open the Codex.

Jessica came up behind him as he worked, with a big smile on her face when she saw him with that Codex page back up. He just gave her a squinty-eyed look. She gave him a dreamy-eyes smile.

"Have a rough night last night?" she asked him coyly.

"I got… *some* sleep," he shined her on. She chuckled. John went back to his reading.

John found what he was looking for in the Special Forces engineering file. *Holy crap! Will you look at that? This thing has its own fusion reactor and a control panel on the wall.* That's funny. He didn't remember any control panel, and he looked that room over real good. Maybe the control panel was hidden. He would have to go see. Then he noticed that for all that did show on the engineering drawings, there was no ring. In fact, what showed instead was a note. "For future use," it read. *Well, somebody used it.* A mystery this good just could not wait, so back he went.

On his way back to the secret room, he met up with Mariah, just going for breakfast.

"Are you going back to bed?" she asked him.

"Hell, no. Sophie and I found a new convoluted room last night. I am going to check it out," he told her enthusiastically. Mariah wasn't exactly awake yet, so he could have told her that he was going roratan hunting, and that would have made just as much sense to her at the moment.

"Okay. Have fun," she told him, turning back to the mess for her tea and oatmeal. When she got there, Jessica was getting a cup of tea.

"Just getting up?" Jessica asked her. Mariah just smiled all dreamy-eyed.

"Rough night?" Jess asked in a low voice.

"Mm, yes. In a good way," Mariah confided in her.

Jessica smiled. "Yeah, in a good way," she agreed.

~

John ran his hand high up by the sensor. He heard the sound of the door opening, so he stepped through. The lights came up. He walked over to where the control panel showed on the engineering drawings, but he couldn't see anything at all there. Then he ran his hand over the wall to see if he could feel anything.

[Good Morning, Captain,] came up in his Mindlink. Aha! This system was tied into the main network. It recognized him as the captain of the vessel.

[Main Menu,] he told it. The system displayed the top-level functions in alien pictographs.

[English,] he commanded, but the screen did not change.

His Mindlink told him that there was optical network in the ring room. He pictured Jessica's naked backside to bring up the alien files. He was getting very good at that. Good thing Mariah didn't know. She would pitch a fit. Anyway, he found the label he was looking for – Translation Anoza / English. He plugged in the first symbol and got back 'Space.' Hm. He would have to look at that later. He was sure that the second symbol looked familiar as he plugged that one in. 'Matter,' it returned. That was why it looked so familiar -- it was. It appeared every time that particular word was used in his reading beyond the tesseract.

From there, he explored the Matter Menu deeper. It had several branches that he had no clue what they were for. Then he found one labeled 'Restore.' He selected that path to find himself looking at four pictures – Mariah Jane Harrington, Jessica Ann Miller, Jane Marie Schultz, and Henry James Merritt.

Restore? Restore what? What is this all about? How 'restored' would they be? From everything else in the Codex files, he had learned to drop a question mark on an item to get a definition or more information. He dropped a question mark on 'Restore.'

[Restore – to convert a current image back into its original biological form.]

Wow. Convert them all back to their original biological form? Now there was a heavy thought. He supposed that there would have to be some very serious consequences to that, so this was not something to be taken lightly nor done without a lot more consideration. Neither did he want to take a chance of screwing up something this important. With all that he was currently in the middle of, he surely did not need to be dealing with 'consequences' right here, right now either. Oh boy, would this ever make some deep brain stew! John shut the ring down and meandered back to the bridge, deep in thought.

~

The problem with Mariah was that the gears in her head were constantly turning and churning over one problem or another. Some of them were important, but some of them were important only to her. She was still in a total dither over Union companies being used by the Syndicate to make war materials for their own hired mercenaries. That one really stuck in her craw. But, you would say that the war was over, so that should be old business, and you would be right… but not to Mariah.

John helped Mariah set up a Merc quantum-com and display in the lounge so that Kira and Nomi could maintain contact with Ishmael to see how he was doing with his fellow castaways. That was certainly its primary use, but in the course of doing that, Kira also ran across individual groups of mercenary ships that had scattered into the far outworlds at the end of the war rather than be captured.

There was one mercenary group, in particular, that was currently looking for a lost convoy of freighters. They were being very persistent in their demands for information from everyone to whom they talked.

[Did you hear that?] Mariah asked John privately.

[Yes, I did,] he answered.

[They want those freighters pretty bad,] she noted. [I just know those freighters have to be full of Union-made technology parts for their damned mercenary war machine.]

[I would imagine so. You know, the more I listen to them asking about it, the more it reminds me of an old battle. It sounds so familiar.]

[Can you look it up and see?] she asked him, but he was already looking through the copy of his old fighter logs over the network.

[I found it! A couple of full squads of Echo-3C fighters set an ambush for that convoy,] he told her. [We jumped them all right, but they had a full Merc fighter escort. We lost a lot of ships to stop that convoy. It must have been a high-value target at the time.]

[How did you stop those freighters?] Mariah asked.

[We just put one engine out of commission on each freighter, as I recall.]

[What happened to their crews?] Mariah probed further.

[There were no crews. They were robot freighters.]

[What happened to the cargos?]

[Geez, I don't rightly know. Nothing, I would imagine. No one had the capability, the time, or the inclination to go all the way back out there to get the cargos during the war, I imagine. Oh, now I see what you mean. It could be seriously bad if the mercenaries find those freighters and get those cargos now.]

[More lives will be lost for no damned reason whatsoever,] she surmised.

[The mercenaries will never find them; even looking in their own waypoints will do them no good. We jumped those ships in open space, way off the normal spaceways,] John told her.

[But you could find them again?] Mariah asked.

[I have the coordinates of that battle,] he confirmed from his log. [They are a couple of years old, so you will have to interpolate where the freighters would be now. When you do, send the new coordinates to Jessica so she can plot us a detour home. We will go take a look-see for ourselves. Maybe we can do something to prevent them from getting those cargos.]

[Okay,] Mariah decided with a smile on her face. [I am good with that.]

[Then that's the plan,] John set the task [When we are done with the mission to rescue Kira's dad, we will go out to the freighters next.] Whatever! Let's just add that to rescuing Mercs and that new batch of brain stew that he had cooking on the back burner. Well, whoever said life would be simple? Shoot 'em.

CHAPTER FOUR
One in a row.

John and Jessica made orbit right above the mercenary base very quietly, with all transponders off. The stage was set for Kira to call her father.

"Father," she called him over the quantum-com. "The time has come."

"We are as ready as we are going to be," he told her to indicate that only he and Lucia were set with this. There was still a problem with Rhianna, and who knows what with Kiroc.

Two ships dropped from orbit and headed for the Merc base, the Tesseract, and Lisa. Kip followed but held back from landing, providing close air support as might be needed. The other three M-4s would hold in orbit for now as backup.

Jessica and Lisa landed side-by-side, setting the ships gently down right in the middle of the base's landing pads. The front gangway went right down, and John emerged unarmed but in his recon armor. Much to his relief, Ishmael and Lucia came out of the main building with Rhianna bound. Rhianna struggled against them despite her bonds, but Ishmael was just too big for her.

John signaled Kira and Nomi with a silent hand wave. They ventured out from behind him slowly at first, but then went running over to Ishmael. Luke and Sam backed up John the whole time from just inside the gangway but were glad to see that there would be no shooting required. Well, maybe not glad, but okay with it.

"Wow," Luke commented to Sam as they followed John down the gangway. "Look at this place. You can't even tell that we shot the crap out of it and left it in shambles."

"We surrender," Ishmael told John. They shook hands. That was the easy part. Luke put a prisoner necklace onto Rhianna, and that was the end of her fighting them. Oh, she tried alright, only to find herself battling her own body for control. That's how those things worked.

"I don't know where Kiroc is," Ishmael told John after they shook hands.

[John! Red Alert!] Kip called as he flew in low overhead. Kip knew exactly where Kiroc was. Kip fired on the pulse-cannon walker as it approached the main gate of the base at a full run. He took the walker down just barely before it crashed the main gate. When Luke and Sam went to investigate, they found it empty. Kiroc had run it at them by remote control as a decoy.

While they all were distracted, Kiroc did manage to sneak around them. Using their temporary confusion as cover, he ran full-out to what he perceived as a friendly: The M-4 with the open gangway. He ran inside shouting, "Close the gangway! Take off!" but he was in for a real surprise. Lisa's maintenance android suddenly came to life, grabbed the pulse-pistol out of Kiroc's hand, and crushed it. He then zip-tied Kiroc's wrist to the bulkhead, but Kiroc was not about to give up so easily. He began fighting the android for everything he was worth.

Kiroc was in for yet another surprise – Lisa. Mariah had modified the M-4 copilots, making them all full-blown techno. Kiroc quickly found himself fighting both Lisa and her android. To Kiroc's credit, he still managed to hold his own… until Luke and Sam showed up. Sam put his lights out with one punch. The next thing Kiroc knew, he woke up with a prisoner necklace on.

Even after all of that, John and Ishmael still tried to reason with Rhianna and Kiroc, but neither of them would hear a word of it. That left John with no other choice; the two prisoners were led away and confined to rooms on the Tesseract until they returned to Panara-5. There, they would be handed over to Union Fleet. As a secondary precaution to the prisoner necklaces, John also set the ship's security to block them at every portal while Mariah processed Ishmael's and Lucia's surrenders through Union Fleet via the quantum-com.

That part of this mission was complete, but Sophie would not rest until she knew how her people had fared in her absence. Mariah had the lead on this. She put all of the ship's active sensors to work and found the tribe at almost the same place as their last encounter. John took the Tesseract up and over, setting her gently down in a clearing next to their camp.

The gangway was not all the way down before Sophie scampered out to greet her tribe. There were joyous hugs and the rubbing of cheeks together and everyone talking excitedly in Chietta.

"Where is Katop?" Sophie asked them.

"Katop is gone," Mahtar answered. "When he sent you away, everyone was very angry with him. So, we all took a vote and banished him. I am chief now."

"Did you come home to stay?" someone in the crowd asked.

"Oh no," she told them all. "I am Ahmtoko now, and my Ka needs me. My whole new tribe needs me. I had to teach them how to howl, and I have to find all the special places for them. I have a sister now and a new mother, too. I am so fortunate. I eat every day."

Like a lot of Union Fleet's idealistic laws, quarantining worlds with their own indigenous pre-spacefaring people was a totally impractical flop. Sophie's world was a prime example of exactly why – evil humans simply overran it. That is exactly what the Mercs had done, and now Mariah was determined that would never happen again to Sophie's people.

How many indigenous people on how many other worlds had already been driven into extinction by evil, greedy humans? Mariah only knew in her heart that would not happen here. This was their chance to make a difference.

"Come with me," Sophie told her tribe. "I have a big surprise for all of you." She led the whole tribe to the now-abandoned Merc base. This time the security system allowed them all to pass, as Ishmael had reset it. In the shelter of the base, the tribe would have the best chance to thrive. There was not only the security of the base's force fields and electric fences, but also a working Medlab with a full artificial doctor, weapons to protect themselves, and pulse-cannon walkers should the growls return. There were buildings to keep them warm and dry against even the most terrible storms.

Luke and Sam trained the tribe on all of the weapons. Most importantly, they had to learn to run the pulse-cannon walkers in case the growls came back. Over the next few days, the tribe settled in, and Sophie was happy that everything that could be done to ensure her people's survival had been done. Best of all, there were the androids to maintain it all for many years to come.

Sophie even managed to get Ketra, an old friend, started down the path of learning. Ishmael set her up with access to the computers. Mariah downloaded her extensive English-Chietta language database to enable the comprehensive teaching software in Ketra's own native language. The teaching software would bring Ketra up to modern educational standards as quickly as she could be taught. Ketra would become the first of her people on this world with a modern education. The hope was for more to follow, but that would be up to them to decide.

"You do know," John told Sophie after a long day, "that any time you want to come home for a visit, we can bring you."

"Well, I might want to come home sometime for another visit, but I will never leave you." She gave him a great big hug and a kiss. She meant every word of that.

"I love you, too. We are staying right here for now until you tell me that you are ready to leave," he told her.

"Maybe tomorrow," she decided. "That way, I can say goodbye to everybody."

~

When they did leave, Sophie sat on the bridge and watched her beloved homeworld disappear behind them with a smile on her face, on Ka's lap, in the warmth of his embrace. Mariah and Aunt Jessica watched with her, as did Emma. It was a happy visit. It would be a warm memory that Sophie would cherish for a long time. And should she grow a little curious, now she could call Ketra on the quantum-com.

Mariah got online to Union Fleet through the quantum-com. She listed Ketra's quantum-com address in the official Union Fleet database for this world, Chorom in the native Chietta language. Mariah listed the Chietta as its indigenous people, so there could no longer be any excuse for Union Fleet to allow bullies or thieves to move in and take over this world as the Mercs had done. Mariah listed herself as their Chief Advocate, so she could ward off any sham legal attempt to do the same.

~

Jessica set course for the freighters. Mariah ran the interpolations from John's old data to see where the freighters should be now. That, in turn, let Jessica refine the course that would take six days, plus or minus adjustments.

While they closed on those freighters, John and Kip spent some pleasant hours with Ishmael discussing their mutual interest – exploring deep space. Ishmael turned out to be the nicest guy. Deep space exploration was his passion, too.

The whole time, Lucia felt like a fifth wheel. However, she was content to spend time talking to Luke and Sam, listening to Jessica's old Earth music, and sitting in the lounge sipping some of Mariah's proper pilgrim wine, thinking about what she would be doing next with her life. She rather fancied the idea of just traveling for a while.

Mariah and Jessica liked Nomi, but she was very quiet, not at all like the other women on board, even her own daughter, Kira. One thing that she was happy to discuss at length was her people, the Mercs.

"Union people call us 'mercenaries,' but we consider that a derogatory term. We call ourselves 'Mercs' because we recognize the mercantile nature of mankind's existence and are determined that each and every person deserves their fair share of it," Nomi told the other women. "In the Union, the big corporations own everything and reap all of the profits. That is not so in Merc society. The workers own the enterprise, and all share in its profits equally. We elect our leaders just like you do, but we also get rid of them just as quickly when they fail to lead us to profit. No society is perfect, however. We found that out when our leaders decided to maximize profits by siding with the Syndicate. Now we all know the consequences of that."

"Maybe you can find a happy medium in the outworlds then," Mariah suggested. "There are plenty of communally organized businesses in the outworlds where the workers do own the business themselves. The Union has no quarrel with that."

"Really? Well, if that is so, maybe we can start over and be happy," Nomi decided.

"Let me get you started with some study materials on how that is organized under Union laws, so that you can see it for yourself. I believe there are also some good references with videos on several communes that have been very successful over the years."

That made Nomi happy. She could live the way she knew, even on a Union world.

While the men talked, Lucia sipped wine, and Nomi studied, Mariah's ever-working, gears-moving mind simply would not sit back and let her relax. Her endless curiosity only added fuel to the ever-burning bonfire in her mind.

[Jess, did John say anything to you about that new convoluted room that he and Sophie discovered?]

[No, but Sophie told me all about it. There is this huge ring in it,] Jess remembered.

[Come on! Let's go see for ourselves,] Mariah encouraged her fellow snoop. Yeah, right. Like either one of them needed any encouragement to snoop.

[I'm game,] Jessica agreed. So, off they trotted, to see the room for themselves. Jessica led the way to the end of that passageway. There was nothing but a blank wall. Mariah looked at Jessica as if she was crazy.

[Sophie said that the Captain had to run his hand across the top to open the door,] Jessica remembered. So that is what she did. They heard the portal open but saw nothing. Jessica had learned well from her fellow free spirit, Sophie. She refused to believe her eyes and simply stepped right through the invisible portal. Mariah, not one to be left standing there, followed quickly on Jessica's heels. When the lights came up, the two snoops stood in awe of the huge ring.

"What do you think it does?" Jessica asked Mariah, who appeared to be looking at the walls. Mariah ran her hand ever so gently over the walls to see if she could find anything.

"I don't know," Mariah said without looking back at Jessica. Mariah was looking for clues as to what the ring did. She knew that somewhere here, there had to be some kind of controls for it. Then Mariah accidentally put her hand on the control panel. It recognized her.

[Mariah Jane Harrington,] it put up on her display and brought her to that spot in the ring menus. All of the text was in Anoza pictographs, but it's not as if she would let a little thing like that stop her from snooping. Oh no, not for one second. She selected her own picture to see what it knew about her while Jessica looked over the ring.

To Jessica's surprise, the ring suddenly came alive. She took a quick step back. A shimmering wall of light formed inside the ring. It was like the surface of a calm pool of iridescent water. What Jessica did not see was that the ring had shut Mariah's artificially intelligent processor down. The next thing Jessica knew, a stark-naked Mariah stepped out of the shimmering wall of the ring. Mariah, discovering herself stark-naked, covered up as best she could with her hands and looked frantically around for her clothes. She spotted them in a pile on the floor, next to the control panel, so she ran over there to put her clothes back on.

Jessica came over to help her, but in doing so, she leaned on the wall, putting her hand right onto the control panel.

[Jessica Ann Miller,] it recognized her and put her picture up on her display. Before Mariah could say a word to warn her, Jessica selected the picture. The next instant, Jessica suddenly dematerialized. Her clothes fell to the floor where she had been standing. The ring had shut Jessica's artificially intelligent processor down to restore her. Moments later, Jessica stepped out of the shimmering wall of light inside the ring just as naked as Mariah had, but unlike Mariah, she really didn't care. She walked calmly over to the control panel and put her clothes back on.

In the meantime, all hell broke loose on the rest of the ship. When the ring shut Jessica's AIU down to restore her, the AIU OFFLINE alarm went off on the bridge, sending John into a total dither and a panic. He went scrambling to the bridge to see what the hell was wrong.

[Mariah! Mariah, I need you on the bridge, on the double!] John called her.

[Network Error. Mariah not found.]

OH SHIT!! Not only was Jessica offline, but so was Mariah?! His next scramble brought him to the computer bay. John carefully called up and executed the combination of moves from the Captain's Tablet to get Mariah's artificial intelligence processor panel open, only to confirm his worst fears. OH CRAP! Mariah's artificial intelligence processor was indeed down.

"I am so screwed!"

"What's wrong?" Mariah asked him from the door.

He turned around and hugged her. "Dear Lord! I thought I lost you."

"No. I am fine… I think." But she definitely looked dazed by the whole experience.

Jessica stood right behind Mariah, with that same dazed look on her face.

John looked at the two of them and then looked at their AI processors. They were both standing right there in front of him. Then he looked at the atomic field projector overhead. Its green LED indicated that it was on standby. So then, how the hell were they standing right there in front of him? That should not be possible.

[John! John!] Kip called him through the network. [What's wrong? Rachel says that Jessica shows as offline. Did you all have a computer crash over there?]

[Yes, we did. Give me a minute to sort it all out.]

"What did you two do?" he asked, as though he would actually get a straight answer from either one of them. They just looked at each other.

"I am not exactly sure," Mariah answered. "One minute I was standing there, and the next, I was walking out of the ring stark naked. My clothes were on the floor, so I put them on."

"Yeah. That's what happened to me too," Jessica agreed.

"Standing there? Standing where?" he asked them.

"In the new convoluted room," Jessica answered.

"Aw shit!" did not adequately express what he was thinking at that moment. He didn't know exactly how they did it, but they both got themselves restored, and this was exactly why he was afraid of restoring them while they were in the middle of a mission – serious consequences. *Whatever!* John's logical mind once more slowly returned.

"Jessica, I need you on the bridge right away," he told her, but they all went to the bridge. Jessica took her copilot's seat, but from there she was lost.

"I don't have any of my displays. Where is my network access?" Jessica asked.

"This is not going to work," John said out loud what he was thinking. He used his own Mindlink to call up the next waypoint and execute the jump.

"She needs a Mindlink," John said to Mariah, more thinking out loud. "You are going to need one too. I have some in stores."

[Hack, emergency! Bring me two Mindlinks from stores, on the double.] While that was happening, John moved them one more time, to the next waypoint.

A couple minutes later, Hack brought him the Mindlinks. The two small boxes held what appeared to be small gold dots. He took the first one and put it on the back of Jessica's head, right onto her scalp. It moved itself around to the correct spot and started to grow its own connections to her brain. While he did the same to Mariah, Jessica's new Mindlink logged her into the network.

Even so, Jessica still struggled to get them to their next waypoint.

Take the next step. Solve the next problem. Now that Jessica was flesh-and-blood human, he was going to need a full-time artificial copilot up and running.

[Mariah, I need you to get the artificial copilot back up and running,] he told her, not thinking at all of the consequences of that.

Mariah worked on the artificial copilot while John and Jessica got them ten more waypoints down course. Jessica was still struggling. John had to mostly pilot the ship himself.

[Hello, I am Angel,] the copilot finally announced when Mariah was done. She looked to be all of thirty, perfectly proportioned, brown hair and deep brown eyes. She was eye candy for sure. Someone had designed her to be that way.

"Would you believe that when I first fired her back up, she actually thought that she was Jessica?" Mariah told John.

"Aw shit. I should have thought of that." *What else could possibly go wrong right now and make this worse?* John asked himself in despair.

"The crash must have confused her. Well, we couldn't have that now, could we?"

"Hell, no," Jessica agreed. "Only I am me."

Oh, really? John questioned that along with his own sanity.

"So, I had to restore Angel to her old self again. That way, there will be no confusion," Mariah told John and Jessica as if that was obvious.

"Oh, yeah? To who? I am already confused," John complained. *Hey! Wait a minute,* John thought to himself. *Mariah doesn't remember that the artificial copilot actually was Jessica? Even scarier, Jessica doesn't remember that she was the artificial copilot. What's wrong with that picture? And who the Hell is Angel?*

[John, what's up with the new copilot? What happened to Jessica?] Kip asked him through the network. [Rachael is in a panic over here.]

[Oh, I am fine. Thank you, Rachel,] Jessica cut in, [but the artificial copilot processor crashed. Then she came back up confused. The poor girl thought that she was me. Can you feature that? But Mariah restored her. So, now she is back to being her old self again.]

Well, there you go! That pretty much said it all!

[Huh? I am confused,] Kip told John.

[You're confused? I am confused, and I live here. Anyway, it looks to me like we just added Angel to the crew of the Tesseract… or restored her… or whatever the hell just happened. I think I need a beer,] John replied. Jane brought him a Habston lager.

[Angel, please take the helm,] John told her. [Jess, go get yourself a good night's sleep. We can start over tomorrow morning.] Mariah and Jessica left John with Angel on the bridge.

[I am confused,] Angel told John after they left. [I have been with the Tesseract since day one. The last I remember, we jumped into a dense filament of space. The next thing I knew was when Mariah woke me back up just a few minutes ago.]

[Angel, that jump was several years ago. A lot has happened since then. I bought this ship from Union Fleet after the war. We are a private, family ship now. Your nav program has been corrected to use the proper eleven-dimensional equations outlined in the Codex, so we can jump right through dense filaments of space safely now.]

[And like every Captain before you, you need to be certain that I am up to my task,] Angel told him bluntly but with a smile.

[I wouldn't be worth a crap as a captain if I didn't,] John replied just as bluntly.

Angel just smiled and flew the ship over the next few hours with the same attention to detail that he had come to expect with Jessica at the helm. In fact, if he closed his eyes, he couldn't tell that it was not Jessica flying the ship.

[Goodnight, Angel,] he told her as it got late. [I am going to bed.]

[Goodnight, Captain,] she replied with a smile as he walked off.

[Iyo?] Angel inquired over the network.

[*I am with you.*]

[I have a new captain,] Angel told her, worried.

[*I chose Leaf in the Wind to save us. He found you. I am well pleased.*]

[Leaf in the Wind?] Angel asked.

[*Leaf in the Wind,*] Iyo confirmed, but then she was gone.

"Leaf in the wind," Angel repeated. Iyo chose him, but Angel was curious. While everyone else slept, Angel flew the ship and read the logs. That is how she discovered that the copilot logs in her absence were all written by Jessica -- as the artificial copilot! And there was a lot more than just ship's operation in those logs. Thanks to Mariah and Jessica, the logs read like a personal diary.

John got up at his usual 07:00 and went to the mess for some java. It was as if his brain stew had been stirred with a hand grenade. The way he saw it, he had no choice now but to cancel any new ops until all of the current 'consequences' were resolved. He felt better already. He had a plan. He was about to go up to the bridge to have Angel change course for Panara-5 when Jessica came into the mess looking all dreamy-eyed. That looked a lot more like his old Jessica.

"How are you doing today?" he was almost afraid to ask.

"Much better," she told him. "I was very confused yesterday, definitely not myself."

"You and Mariah were both pretty confused yesterday," he agreed.

"Well, your girl Jessica is back with the program today," she assured him with a big smile. "My new Mindlink is totally up and running. I have all of my old screens back. I am rip-roaring and ready to go."

"Am I ever relieved to hear that," he told her with a big hug.

"Ooh, that's a nice way to start my day," Jessica whispered into his ear.

"Hey! What the hell is going on here?" Mariah complained as she came into the mess.

His Mariah was back to being a total pain in the ass butt-crack. He grabbed her too and hugged them both. They both thought he was nuts, but he was sure that he was the only sane one on the ship.

"I was going to ask how you are feeling today, but you sound perfectly fine to me," he told Mariah.

"And just exactly what do mean by that?" She was still riled and still a royal pain in the ass. As far as John could tell, his Mariah was fine.

"After yesterday, I was very worried about you two. You were both dazed and confused. I was about to cancel this op to get the freighters and just go home."

"Cancel the op? Oh, no! No damned way!" Mariah was about to get herself all wound up.

"Wait a minute. I don't need to do that now. You are both fine today," he told Mariah as if that answer would save him now.

Mariah hit him in the shoulder.

"Ow! Hey! What the hell was that for?" he complained.

"Fine… My ass! I'll give you fine!" she shook her clenched fist at him.

"Yes," he agreed with her, "you do have a fine ass."

"You wipe that big, shit-eating grin off your face, or you are going to get hit again," she threatened him with a clenched fist.

"Hey!" Sophie scolded her from the portal, "No hitting! He's my Ka."

"Sometimes I think he aggravates her on purpose," Emma told Sophie quietly.

"I know, but I still have to defend him," Sophie confessed to Emma.

Somehow, everything was back to normal. Okay. You and I both know this isn't normal, but it was as normal as it got for them.

Ishmael and Nomi woke up and came into the mess just in time to miss all of that. They had no clue here what was normal on this ship either, so finding everyone in the mess, quietly having some breakfast, didn't seem at all out of place. Luke and Sam were laughing and joking with Kira and Gina. Even that could have been construed as normal too.

"John," Ishmael addressed him before he had a chance to get up from the table. "You saved my daughter, and then you came all this way to rescue me. I didn't know how to properly thank you, but now I know how much you would appreciate a copy of this." He passed John his tablet across the table. It contained the original personal star charts and database of seven generations of deep space explorers, beginning with the famous original navigator, Ishmael Tobruk himself.

"Oh, wow. I sure would!" John answered, not about to pass up this opportunity. His eyes lit up like a little kid at Christmas, but this was a job for Mariah. He looked at her.

[Oh yeah! Wouldn't you just know that a goodie for you is nothing but more work for me!]

He gave her his best boyish grin.

[Oh, cut that out! Okay. But I trust nothing, and then I don't trust that,] Mariah told John privately. Mariah had to pull every trick in the book out of her butt to extract the data from Ishmael's tablet and merge the records into their own database. Her caution was not for naught, either. Merc databases were purposely 'rigged' to prevent just what she was doing. Finding the bugs and killing them was no simple task either.

What did surprise Mariah, though, was the number of records that were different in the Merc database – over a million stars, planets, and other details had been doctored or removed altogether from the Union star charts by the Syndicate's conspirators so many years ago.

But the real kicker to all of this was the fact that this was only the surface level of all the data that Syndicate had hidden so well over many years. It was generally taken for granted that there was yet another layer, hidden even deeper, known only to the Syndicate themselves. Even the most trusted Mercs didn't have that data in their star charts.

Mariah was still upset that John's projects always made work for her. She did know, however, that John would find endless hours of pleasure going through seven generations of deep space explorers' own personal records. Mariah just could not understand how he could possibly find that interesting. To her, it was more like watching paint dry.

While Mariah was still busy, John and Jessica went to the bridge to find Angel sitting in the copilot's seat. Angel smiled at them. John didn't have the heart to just boot her out of her seat. It was time for some decision-making.

"Here is how this is going to work," John told his two copilots. "I am going to have Hack help me rebuild the engineer's workstation over for my own personal use. It will become the captain's workstation. Jessica, I am promoting you to pilot. Angel, you are now the full-time copilot. Any questions?"

Jessica was beaming. Being the pilot was way better than being the copilot. Angel was good with that, too. The copilot's seat had been her rightful place since day one. Her new captain obviously recognized that.

"That frees up the captain for higher-level command functions," John concluded.

"What did I miss?" Mariah asked from the portal as she entered.

"I was promoted to pilot!" Jessica informed her. Angel just sat there and smiled.

"I am rebuilding the engineer's workstation over into a proper captain's workstation," John informed her. "Jessica is an excellent pilot and is usually flying the damned ship anyway. That will free me up to work on higher-level command functions. I just need to go get Hack started rebuilding this workstation for me. I have a definite idea of what I want." John linked all of that directly to Hack, so he could get started.

John left the ladies to their own reorganizing while he went to the ring room to try to figure out exactly what his two snoops had done to get themselves restored. He put his hand on the control panel on the wall.

[Good morning, Captain,] it recognized him right away and put the Main Menu up for him. John went down the Matter menus to the Restore menu, but this time only found two pictures: Jane Marie Schultz and Henry James Merritt. That pretty much confirmed that the girls had snooped their way in here and somehow managed to get themselves restored. He could put that much to rest now, but it also taught him a lesson – restore Jane and Hack later, when he had the time to deal with the consequences.

Chapter Five
A matter of mass confusion.

John sat in his new captain's workstation and made himself comfortable.

[Codex,] he sent down the network expecting to next have to recall the picture of Jessica's naked backside, but now the Codex recognized him and simply open up. In a way, that was a bit of a disappointment.

John carefully re-read the Codex file on matter and found that to also be a complete description of the functions of the field coil in the ring room. He set himself to the use of the aliens' proper name – the Anoza. That is who they are. They don't seem so alien when you call them by name. He was finding that out. He knew what they meant now by the Anoza use of the word 'moons' to describe the complete digital image of a person. In fact, he found it to be a beautiful metaphor.

[I don't know your name,] John addressed the anoza spirit somewhere deep in the bowels of his ship, [but I will call you friend. I must admit that restoring Mariah and Jessica sure had its moments, and you can take that to the bank, but you were right. It is a beautiful thing. Right now, I am trusting you with Mariah and Jessica not remembering being artificial. I figure that you must have your reasons for that. I sure hope you don't mind that I wait to restore Jane and Hack until I get home. It would be way too confusing to do that right now. After all, I am only human. All of this is very overwhelming to me.]

That said, it was time to set his mind onto the present op and move on.

~

The Tesseract approached the derelict freighters directly until Jessica announced, "We have company out there. I am picking up a lot of long-range sensor sweeps from at least two Merc light cruisers. They are seriously intent on finding those freighters."

"Sneak in, sneak out, is what we need to do. We know where they should be," John told Jessica. Mariah checked all of her calculations and worked with Jessica to get it on the tactical display while Angel flew the now finely intricate course. The course details were all communicated to Kip's copilot, Rachel, and the M-4s and flown as an interlocked-field formation.

The Tesseract group arrived on Mariah's minimum estimated drift coordinates but found nothing. Using nothing more than the passive sensors, Mariah looked ahead of them for the freighters, but that was a longshot. Jessica and Angel flew the whole course but found nothing.

"There is a filament of dense space that does not show up on our Union charts that does show up in Ishmael's data," Mariah discovered. "Let's see if that makes a difference." And it did. Over the next few hours, they searched the new course and quickly found themselves approaching the freighters from behind. It looked a lot worse than John remembered, but that battle was several years ago. Only two of the three freighters were still mostly intact. The other one was a vast field of debris.

The freighters were skeletons of what you would expect of a starship. Along the central backbone, spaceworthy shipping containers were attached. At the front end of the freighter were all of the controls. These were robot freighters, so there was no need for life support or human habitation. Even the engines were mounted externally to the space-frame.

John looked at this task differently now that he could see it. On one freighter, only a single engine had been damaged. John designated that 'freighter-one' and the other as 'freighter-two.' There appeared to be a lot more damage on freighter-two. He would need to get up close to find out just how bad that was.

[Lisa,] John directed her, [I need you to go over to freighter-one and get connected to its network. Can you do that?]

[I will try.]

"Mariah, when she gets connected, I need you to get us a manifest of what is in each shipping container."

"I can do that… I think," she replied. "What are we looking for?"

"Engines. Find me some engines to work with. That is what I need."

[Ann,] John addressed another one of his M-4 copilots, [I need you to go see if you can connect to the network on freighter-two. Can you do that, please?]

[I will give it a go,] she replied.

[First, try its wi-fi. If that does not work, see if you can use your front manipulator arms to grab a fiber-optic network cable,] Mariah coached her.

As those two M-4s worked their tasks, Mariah and Jessica coached them along. All John could do now was to let the ladies do their thing. He hovered over every bit of it but forced himself not to kibitz. At the same time, Jessica watched one mercenary light cruiser, in particular, that was generally headed toward them. They would be fine if that cruiser stayed on his present course, but that was a big 'if.'

The original battle that took these freighters down was far enough off of the normal spaceways, but now the derelict ships were drifting back toward a mercenary waypoint, according to Ishmael's charts. The clock was ticking as John set about to figure out what he could do. Lisa connected just fine to freighter-one. It held mostly containers of engines and artificial intelligence modules. Ann connected into freighter-two only after ripping apart some panels to find the network fiber optic cable.

"Oh shit," Mariah said quietly. "No wonder they want this freighter. There are over 100 quantum torpedoes on it. We have to get those." Mariah was morally opposed to these terrible weapons of mass destruction, so now the decisions were about to get hard to make.

[Ciara,] John addressed another of his M-4 copilots, [I need you to go fetch me one of the containers from freighter-two with the quantum torpedoes. Mariah will release it for you.]

"Mariah, release one container of quantum torpedoes so Ciara can bring it to us."

Mariah did as he requested but looked hard and questioningly in his direction.

"Trust me, I know what I am doing," he told her in a loud whisper. "I will have the last say but only if and when necessary."

Ciara brought the container and positioned its airlock to the Tesseract's airlock. Jessica locked onto it and cycled the airlock. John, Luke, Sam, and Hack hustled for the next two hours to pull all of those quantum torpedoes out of their crates and store them on the Tesseract.

[Have Ciara bring me another container,] John told Jessica and Mariah. Mariah sure wasn't happy at all about any of this, but she would rather not see these terrible things go into the mercenaries' hands either. It was a challenge to her moral opposition to these things to have to do this, let alone to hear that John would even consider using one.

[What are you thinking?] she demanded to know of John now.

[I am going to try to replace the engine on freighter-one with one from their own cargo. I will have to ditch some of the cargo to get all of the containers of quantum torpedoes from freighter-two onto freighter-one. The plan would then be to fly freighter-one the hell out of here, right under their noses. Failing that, I will need all of the ships to take on however many quantum torpedoes we can fit in them, even if that isn't much.]

[What are those quantum torpedoes that you brought on board for?] she asked him pointedly.

[One of them will be used as a last resort to blow up what we can't take away from the mercenaries,] he told her.

[I am good with that, but I am not good with it taking any lives with those damned things.]

[Okay,] John agreed. [We won't take any lives with them,] but he did reserve final judgment on that. [You are in charge of shuffling containers to get all of the quantum torpedoes onto freighter-one while I replace that damaged engine,] he told Mariah.

[Jessica, please call Barbie over. I will use her ship to work on that engine.]

[Barbie? Are you sure? She's a ditz, you know,] Jessica warned him.

[Okay, I'll remember that. In the meantime, get her over here and docked.]

"Of all the copilots for this job, he has to pick Barbie," Jessica complained to Mariah. "She is nice enough, but the girl is a real ditz. I didn't know that an artificial could be a ditz until you made Barbie."

~

Barbie positioned her M-4 to dock with the Tesseract.

[I am docked and locked,] she reported to Jessica when she had. Jessica cycled the airlock. Barbie sat quietly and waited… and worried. She may have been a ditz, but she had a gentle soul. The Captain himself would soon be on board her ship. She was nervous. She hoped she wouldn't do anything dumb to embarrass herself. She knew what the other girls said about her. She just had to concentrate and do exactly what he told her to do.

John's face appeared on Barbie's display. [Hi Barbie.]

[Hi, Captain, I am so happy that you are coming on board my ship.]

[Me too.] He made his way to the airlock and went aboard her ship. He took the pilot's seat and strapped in. She materialized her persona into the copilot's seat. John looked at her. She was a very sweet-looking blond female copilot with blue-green eyes and a smile that lit up the bridge. She moved with a gracefulness that matched her gentle spirit.

[Cycle the airlock, please,] he commanded. She executed.

[Undock,] he commanded, she executed.

[Captain has the helm,] he told her. He flew them quickly over to freighter-one's damaged engine and started pulling it. That should have been an easy job on this skeleton freighter. Just pull three very large pins, but first, he had to pull the fuel lines, a network cable, some control cables, and the power cables. The list went on. Easy my ass.

[Barbie, please record every connection for me so we can be certain to get them all replaced,] he told her, and so they began. Barbie held their position rock solid all the time he worked. She moved the M-4 carefully but only exactly as he commanded. John told Barbie what to label each connection as they went along.

[Left a bit,] he told her at one point. [Okay. Right there. Hold, please.] For as much as Jessica had warned him that Barbie was a ditz, she was doing just fine. She was precisely following his instructions, nothing more, and nothing less. She wasn't anticipating. It was as if he could almost feel her breath on the back of his neck; she was following his commands that closely.

Lisa brought them his new engine before he was ready. She held it back, out of the way as he finally got to the 'pull three large pins' part. That should have been the easy part, except that one of them was stuck. John jury-rigged a pin-puller out of floating debris to finally get the damaged engine free.

Lisa pushed the new engine into place using John's view from Barbie's ship for the very fine last few centimeters. John got the first two pins pushed back in just fine, but wouldn't you know, that damned third pin was going to be a bugger. John looked at the pin. Sure enough, it was just very slightly bent. He held the pin with the left manipulator, heating it just so with a welding torch, trying to get the pin to straighten itself out. It cooperated some but not enough. That forced him to go at the damned thing with a grinder. He kept grinding a little bit at a time and trying the pin until it went into place, but when it finally did go in, the pin was too loose. He had no choice anymore but to weld the damned pin into place now.

"Bandits!" Jessica called over the ship-to-ship. "Three M-3s. They haven't spotted us yet."

That is when Barbie panicked. She froze.

"Barbie dear, are you alright?" John asked her calmly.

"I don't know what to do," she said with a shaky voice. "I don't want to screw up, and then you will be mad at me."

"Barbie, listen only to my voice. Concentrate on what I tell you to do. You will do just fine. Trust me."

"Okay. I will just do exactly what you tell me," she said. "I trust you."

The com came alive as those M-3s spotted the whole salvage operation in progress. He could see by the look on her face that Barbie was almost back to panicking again.

"Don't listen to any of that," he encouraged her very calmly. "You are with me. I know exactly what to do. I am your captain. I will get you through this."

"You know exactly what to do," she repeated, now concentrating on his voice. "You will get me through this. I am trusting you. You are my captain."

"See, I knew you could do it. Now, play me back the engine connections, backward. I need to get this all back connected. While I do that, you watch our back. If you see an M-3 headed our way, put up the rear shields and fire rear pulse-cannons at him, but hold me rock steady so I can get this done. Can you do that for me?"

"Yes. I can do that," she replied. And so, John calmly began the reattachment as if there was no battle about to rage all around him.

The three M-3s came in fast for a hard fly-by and were immediately confused. What they thought they saw was another mercenary group at work here, but mixed in was an Echo-3 and a Union scout-class ship. Mariah got onto the mercenary quantum-com and did her best to convince them that they were interfering with a Merc op in progress. That bought another twenty minutes as the M-3 pilots reported back to their carrier. John used that whole time to methodically work his way back through all of those connections. He tested each one carefully as it was completed. There was no room here for any errors.

The Merc carrier entered near space as Mariah and Jessica scrambled to get the last of the cargo containers with quantum torpedoes attached to freighter-one. Mariah fed freighter-one a whole new course back home to Panara-5 before she called John.

[How goes it?] She asked him quietly. She could see by his face on her display that he was concentrating intently on the last of the engine connections.

[Ten more minutes,] he told her as he made up the fuel connectors. [Does it have a course home?]

[Yes, it does. It's ready to go.]

[Did we get all of the quantum torpedoes?] he asked as he continued.

[Yes, we did, but there are still too many high-value parts left on the other freighter to just leave it.]

[Well, then you know what you have to do.]

[Yes, I do. As long as it won't be killing any people, I can live with that,] she told him reluctantly. What she had to do was to fire a quantum torpedo at it just before they boogied the hell out of here. There was no other choice. It was the only weapon powerful enough to do the whole job, but that didn't make Mariah feel any better about it. No matter what, it still grated on her soul to have to use one.

[I am counting on you,] he told Mariah. [Next step, please, Barbie.]

The carrier launched a full wing of nine M-3s. They obviously knew they would be fighting their own M-4s and were not about to take that lightly. Kip picked right up on that and surprised them with a full-on attack with three M-4s and his Echo-3C. That scattered the formation. The fight was on. Jessica moved the Tesseract in close to cover John.

John worked feverishly on the last few connections as Barbie opened fire on one M-3 that made it past Jessica to harass them.

"Fire a spread ahead of him. Lead him," he encouraged her, and it worked. Barbie started landing rounds on his shields. That forced him to back off. Then a second M-3 managed to get by Jessica, but Lisa was on it and managed to drive it off.

"Very good, Barbie," John complimented her. "See, I knew you could do it. You are doing a fine job."

"The carrier is launching another wing of fighters!" Jessica announced just as John finished his work. John brought up the freighter's engineering panel through its wi-fi and ran an engine diagnostic. It passed! He brought up the freighter's navigation display just as things got dicey. The sky was now full of M-3s, all maneuvering heavily. He initiated the freighter's new course on a five-second countdown.

[Back off now!] he told Barbie. She did exactly that.

[It's done!] John announced as freighter-one lit up its engines and jumped off to its first waypoint. Kip followed the plan. He followed freighter-one to protect it. John took over command of his wing of M-4 fighters and pulled one more big surprise on the Mercs – he attacked the carrier. That drew all of the Merc fighters back to protect it.

[Fire the torpedo!] he told Mariah, but she hesitated. [Come on! Come on! I am drawing them back to the carrier, so you won't kill anybody! Now

Fire the damned torpedo!]

Reluctantly… she fired the torpedo. She was supposed to leave right away after that, but again, she hesitated. John didn't have time to notice. He was working like a mad man on a quantum torpedo of his own. The Merc carrier must have realized at this point that they were in big trouble and started maneuvering heavily.

"Don't flinch," he told Barbie as he worked. "You hold dead nuts onto that carrier. Keep them right in your sights." He loaded the quantum torpedo into his weapons rack and slammed that hatch shut. John took his seat, opened the weapons rack to space, and calmly fired the quantum torpedo directly at the carrier. Total pandemonium broke out. The M-3 fighters trying to protect the carrier all scattered. At the last second, the carrier jumped out… just ahead of a huge flash.

John led his fighters out to their next waypoint. When they arrived, he noticed that Barbie was smiling.

[They call me a ditz, you know,] she told him.

[Well, that's not very nice. You did a flawless job, and you didn't flinch in battle, either. I am very proud of you.]

[Thank you,] she beamed.

John's wing of fighters met up with the Tesseract three waypoints down course. Barbie docked with the Tesseract.

While the airlock cycled, he hugged Barbie and told her, "don't you listen to anybody. You are no ditz. You are pretty special in my book." She hugged him back. He gave her a goodbye kiss on the cheek.

As he exited the M-4 into the Tesseract, Mariah met him, mad as all hell. She was red in the face. "You fired a quantum torpedo at them!" she all but yelled at him.

"Yes, I did," he admitted. "It sure made one hell of a big bang, and I am sure that the flash will be seen for years to come, but it couldn't fracture time-space without this." He took her hand and put a heavy piece of metal into it. She looked long at the piece in her hand.

"You just need to trust me," he reminded her. "I said that I would not kill anyone with a quantum torpedo, and I damned well meant it, and I damned well kept my promise. I just wasn't telling those mercenaries that the damned thing wasn't live anymore. Hell, did you see them scatter when I fired it at them?"

"I sure did. I am sorry. I should have trusted you," Mariah admitted that she was wrong for what had to be the first time in recorded history. He hugged her and kissed her.

"I am sorry, too," Jessica told him from somewhere behind Mariah. "Do I get a hug and kiss now?"

"Sure, why not?"

Mariah gave him the stink-eye, so he made it a friendly kiss, but Jessica was happy anyway.

"Wow, am I ever hungry," John noticed for the first time.

"Barbie didn't feed you?" Jessica asked.

"We didn't have time," John replied.

Jessica rolled her eyes. "You're just protecting her now."

"Barbie is just a simple soul," John rose to her defense. "As much as you told me that she was a ditz, she performed flawlessly. She followed my every command, and she didn't flinch when I told her to charge that carrier full-on. You girls calling her a ditz only hurt her self-esteem. I hope I fixed some of that."

She is still a ditz, Jessica thought to herself as they all went to the mess.

John sat in the mess eating a roast beef sandwich on one of those delish kimmelweck rolls when Ishmael and Nomi came in and sat down.

"What was this all about?" Ishmael wanted to know. They had watched the whole thing play out on the wall-sized 3D displays throughout the ship.

John finished the bite he was working on and put down his sandwich. "It was all about saving a whole lot of lives," he began slowly. "There were these two freighters that were left in deep space, disabled, during the war. One of them was transporting quantum torpedoes."

"Those are terrible weapons, indeed," Ishmael agreed but still looked for more to this answer.

"If I had left them there, your fellow Mercs would have taken them. A lot of good people would have died, but the war is over. No one else needs to die. I am sick of people dying. I took away those terrible weapons so that no one else would die by them."

"But you fired two of them," Ishmael accused him. "How is that not killing?"

"One was fired at the derelict freighter that we could not move. No one was on it."

Mariah put that the part on the table that John had handed to her on his return. "And the other one had this part removed. It could make an immense flash, but it could no longer fracture time-space," she told Ishmael.

"But it sure did fool that carrier commander. You should have seen the mad scramble to get the hell out of there before the damned thing went off," John told Ishmael and Nomi.

A smile crossed Ishmael's face. "We did. I am so happy to be wrong. You are indeed a good man after all, but you are definitely evil in a good way."

"You just need to trust me," he told Ishmael. "When I give my word on something, I mean it, and you can take that to the bank."

"Okay, I will trust you, but first, I need you to explain something to me – making a difference starts with me. Kira told me that. What does it mean?"

The explanation was long. John and Ishmael enjoyed a Habston Lager as they discussed it.

Chapter Six
To be or not to be.

The trip home was going to be a slow one, as they now had to protect a robot freighter that could only do C20 at best. So much for anyone questioning John's sanity for bringing six ships to save four people anymore. Nothing ever worked out the way he thought. So, why should this have been any different?

John decided that Barbie needed to fly his single star along with her transponder ID to indicate his choice of her as his M-4 flagship when he wasn't aboard the Tesseract. The other women copilots could easily take care of themselves, but Barbie needed a leader to follow. That way he could look out for her gentle soul himself. He really did know that Barbie was still a ditz, but he wouldn't hear of anybody calling her that anymore.

"You are smiling, Ka?" Sophie asked him as he sat in his captain's workstation.

"I was just thinking about Barbie," he told her.

"I am very proud of you," she told him with a hug. "You brought harmony to Barbie."

"I hope so," he told her.

"Barbie is happy and proud now. The other copilots don't tease her anymore."

"That makes me happy. She is a gentle soul," he told Sophie.

"I always knew that. I was waiting for someone else to see it too."

~

"I have some good news," Mariah told him as they took their bridge stations after lunch. "When I talked to our friend, Admiral Johnson, she said that she would send a battle group out to meet us. She was laughing like hell and saying something about not cramping your style."

"We saved a lot of lives," John expressed his thoughts. "We made a difference."

"Yes, we did." There was a big smile on Mariah's face too.

~

It all started with a flight of ten Echo-5 fighters and a hard flyby. Everybody flashed their landing lights. Jessica hailed them over the laser-com. After that, ship after ship entered local space until the entire battle group sat out in front of them. The battleship Ticonderoga was a familiar sight to John. It was accompanied by five light cruisers and two fighter carriers. What they had come for was that important.

[Commodore Korbin,] Captain Hamels of the Ticonderoga spoke to John over the laser-com finally, [Admiral Johnson warned me not to cramp your style. What the hell did she send me all the way out here at flank speed to get?]

[How about 100 quantum torpedoes?]

[Good Lord! Where did you find those?]

[I barely snatched them away before a Merc battle group got to them. My XO is sending you a full report. I patched together this skeleton freighter enough to get them this far.]

Over the next few hours, the Union Fleet ships picked up the salvage process. They moved all of the shipping containers to the flight deck of the Ticonderoga. It gave Mariah great pleasure to know that these terrible weapons of mass destruction were back into trustworthy hands of Union Fleet.

The Union was so happy to get these back that Admiral Johnson deposited 10,000 Union dollars per torpedo into the Tesseract's interplanetary bank account. So far, the Union was quickly becoming his best paying customer. Don't get me wrong; the money was good, but sometimes a hug was better.

That freed the Tesseract group to make way for home at their normal C30. Luke was becoming anxious to get back to his Rebecca, Ishmael and his family were anxious to start their new life, and Mariah was actually anxious to get back home, herself. That was new.

More consequences of restoring her?

John sat quietly on the bridge, just watching Jessica and Angel fly the course home. The blouse Jessica wore exposed most of her back. The anoza tattoo, it was gone!

[Jess, what happened to your tattoos?] he asked her.

[Oh? You finally noticed? Men! That damned ring happened to my tattoos!] she complained. [I liked my dragon-birds.]

[I liked your dragon-birds, too,] he agreed.

[Now I am going to have to find a good tattoo artist to replace them when we get home,] she complained.

John thought that was the end of that conversation until he ran into Sophie and Emma in the mess eating their snack.

"What are you thinking so hard about, Ka?" Sophie asked him.

"Oh, just Aunt Jessica's tattoos," he replied. "I miss her dragon-birds."

"She does, too," Emma replied, "but she doesn't remember the symbols down her back."

"I even reminded her that they were like my spots," Sophie added, "but she still didn't remember them at all."

"Consequences," John mumbled to himself. "Everything has consequences."

"It gave them back their scent, though," Sophie confided in him. "Now she and Mom smell like other women."

"Yes, come to think about it now, I did notice that," he admitted to Sophie. He just didn't tell her that he noticed it in the heat of love when Mariah's new scent intoxicated his senses.

~

John was still thinking about all of those consequences the next morning at breakfast when Barbie suddenly popped in. She literally did just that. She reached across the network that extended through all of the ships via the quantum-com and materialized in the mess on the Tesseract.

"Good morning, Captain," she greeted him but then seemed lost for words after that.

"Good morning, Barbie. What brings you to see us this morning?" he asked.

"I was curious," she answered him simply.

He smiled. "Sure, come sit by me while I have my breakfast. Do you want anything?"

She looked at his breakfast burritos and java but didn't quite know what to make of it. John gave her a small taste. Her eyes lit up. It was a bit hot for her. He handed her his fruit juice. She drank that down and smiled.

"Am I bothering you?" she asked, concerned that she might be.

"Heavens, no. It's nice to have company for breakfast," he smiled. "I have to get to my work after breakfast, but you can stay with me until then."

"Oh, good," she said. "I wanted to ask you -- everyone calls you Captain, but you are really a Commodore. Why is that?"

"Commodore is only my military rank, so Union Fleet refers to me by that title, but this is just a family ship. On this ship, I am just Captain. That's all I need to be."

"But the rank of Commodore is also referred to as 'Captain of the Fleet.' Technically, you are in command of all of these ships, so technically you are still a commodore. You are Captain-of-the-Tesseract-Fleet," she reasoned.

"Hm. I never thought of that. Then, just between you and me, we will know that when somebody calls me Captain, that they really mean Captain-of-the-Fleet. It will be our little secret."

Barbie's whole face lit up. That made her happy. She was happy until he stood up. She knew that he had to go see to his work, but she wasn't quite sure about how to say goodbye. John solved that for her. He hugged her and kissed her cheek just the same as he would any other female member of the family. After all, his M-4 copilots were family by now.

"I have to get to work," he said to her.

"Okay, me too," she told him and, pop, she disappeared back across the network to her own ship just as quickly as she had popped in.

As John took his seat on the bridge, he was suddenly struck by the contrast of Barbie, a true techno right from the get-go, and Mariah. Barbie was a natural denizen of the network, coming and going as quickly as looking at you. Her clothes were whatever she materialized along with her persona. Food and drink to her were a novelty. She didn't need a bed to sleep in; she simply went dormant on the network while her backup processor ran her ship.

When Mariah was techno, on the other hand, she wore regular clothes and slept in a regular bed. She ate and drank just like any other biological human. Mariah was techno, and at the same time, she wasn't. Jessica was even more of a conundrum. She wasn't techno at the start, but when she was, she was every bit as 'bio' acting as Mariah. Now he wondered how it was going to work when he restored Jane and Hack. Whatever, it was the right thing to do. The chips would fall where they may.

~

This homecoming was a bit strange. Ishmael and Nomi decided to claim a homestead and settle down right there on Panara-5. Nomi planned to start their own communally organized business. Kira and Gina left to help them get that started. Lucia left in search of a starship to anywhere. Rhianna and Kiroc were handed over to Union Fleet with the hope that Fleet and their fellow Mercs could talk some sense into them.

Luke went back over to Rebecca's place almost the second the gangway went down. Sam was on his own, but he seemed to be okay with that, at least for now.

~

Mariah, Jessica, and John went to the ring room when things calmed down. They carried two boxes of clothes from storage: one marked 'Jane Schultz' and the other marked 'Henry Merritt.' When everyone was ready, John put his hand on the control panel. He carefully worked his way through the menus, to find the picture labeled 'Jane Marie Schultz.' He selected the picture and turned his back to the ring as it came alive.

Jane stepped out of the ring stark naked but found Mariah and Jessica right there, handing her clothes. She was a little dazed at first, but that quickly faded. Jane was much younger than her picture made her look. While she was by no means fat, she was definitely not thin by any stretch of the imagination. Her medium blond hair and shining blue eyes suited her to a tee. Once she was dressed, Mariah escorted her out of the room.

John once more put his hand on the control panel. This time, he selected the picture labeled 'Henry James Merritt.' Henry stepped out of the ring naked to find Jessica and John waiting for him with some clothes. Henry was not quite as dazed as Jane had been. Henry was not at all what John pictured. He was wiry and of average height at best. He had thick dark brown hair and an equally thick Cockney brogue to his speech, which seemed to be flowing out of him incessantly, except that he mostly appeared to be talking to himself. He was happy that Jessica was there.

"How are you doing, Hack, my man?" John asked him.

"I am okay, I think," he answered, "but my name is Henry."

They all gathered in the mess. Jane had her android bring them all some java and tea. Now that was weird. The android he used to refer to as 'Jane' was back to being Jane's helper. That would take quite some getting used to.

"Hack, what do you remember?" John asked him.

"I am pretty clear all the way up to a half hour ago. Then the lights went out. Next thing I knew, I was stepping out of the ring. You and Jessica were there to meet me with some clothes. This java is good. Well, maybe a bit strong. It could use some sugar. Where the hell is Andy?"

"It was about the same for me," Jane told them all. "I think I will feel better when I am back in my kitchen," Jane decided. Sophie came over to Jane and smelled her but said nothing.

"Sophie, little one, I think I have some cookies with your name on them. Come on with me." They left for the galley, Emma trailing behind.

"Yeah," Hack agreed, "I will feel better if I just get back to work, too." He got up and left.

Jessica went off with Hack. Mariah got up and went to make sure that Jane was okay.

John sat there alone for a while, just letting this all seep in.

Sophie and Emma came back from the kitchen and sat down next him. "I like what they did with Jane," Sophie told Emma. "She is much better as a human than she ever was as an android. I just have to get used to her new smell."

"She smells like kitchen," Emma chuckled.

"Yes, some, but she has her own human smell now, too."

"Okay, if you say so," Emma decided. They looked at John.

"I better go make sure the ship is okay," John told the girls as he got up.

[I hope you are happy now,] he told the anoza spirit somewhere in his ship.

My soul sings songs of joy!

CHAPTER SEVEN
Full moon.

John came to the bridge early the next morning to find Angel sitting at her station, quietly reading the ship's logs and reviewing the stored videos at a blistering pace.

[I was a victim of the crash, too,] she said quietly to him.

[Yes, you were. I am sorry. That hadn't occurred to me.]

[So much has changed,] she confided in him. [How did Jessica suddenly become such a good pilot? The last I remember, she was just an average pilot at best.]

[Really? Since my first day, she has flown this ship… exactly the same way you do.]

[But back then, she was the artificial copilot,] Angel said, much to his surprise.

[Yes, she was,] he admitted.

Angel smiled. [Now I know where that came from.]

Now, so did John.

[And Mariah,] Angel continued. [She was always a good Science Officer, but she never did any programming at all. When did that change?]

[The first day, I set foot upon the decks of this ship. Somehow, that changed everything.]

[Yes, indeed. You did.]

Another 'consequence' that really threw John for a loop was the fact that Hack was, in reality, a very highly qualified and credentialed starship engineer. Even more confusing was that Hack was now bossing around the very android that he had once inhabited, as though it were human. He talked to the android while he worked. It was more like he mumbled, so it was difficult to understand if he was actually talking to the android or to himself. Sometimes, it was both. Sometimes, he talked to the ship, not that he realized that the anoza spirit was in there someplace, but to the ship itself, as if the ship had a life of its own.

John could now assign Hack a lot of the tasks that he had been doing himself, but that would leave John with even less to do himself. With Jessica and Angel doing the flying and Hack doing the engineering, he was going to need some serious captain work to keep himself busy. As scarce as real jobs were, he was beginning to become concerned.

In the interim, John bought some seriously high-powered ultraviolet lasers for his next project on the Tesseract and set them aside while he tried to figure out exactly how to apply them. John would never have thought to tell Hack, the android, what he was doing with those lasers, so it never occurred to him to let Hack, the human, know now. What John didn't realize was that those lasers sat there in stores, driving Henry a little crazy every time he looked at them. Oh, boy. That was a short drive.

And, for the record, Henry Merritt did not really like being called 'Hack' at all. And while we are on the subject of what was driving Henry crazy, he sure would rather be doing some real engineering than all of this ships' maintenance that John had assigned him. More things that added to Henry's crazy were those damned Merc M-4 fighters.

John found Henry looking over his M-4s one fine morning.

"They could be really fine craft had they not all been built by the lowest bidder," John commented to Henry. Well, that was all he had to say to set Henry off. Henry started listing all of the things he would do to remedy that, pointing them all out using Barbie's ship as the example. John was very impressed as he followed Henry around the ship and let Henry ramble on until it sounded like he ran out of steam. Now, you have to know, that took some real patience on John's part.

"I need you to make all of our ships into somebody's worst nightmare," John told Henry. "In addition to everything you just told me on the M-4s, I need you to add the latest outworld rail-gun cannons and outworld missiles. I need all of our M-4 fighters to get the same energy reflective skin that the Tesseract has. How long would it take to get all of that done?" John asked Henry, much to his surprise.

"Oh, maybe a month or so to finish all the work on all of the ships," Henry ventured, "but to do that, I will have to rent some androids to multiply our workforce. That would let me work on all of the ships at once. Would you like me to add multiple rail-gun cannons and missiles to the Tesseract, too, while I am at it?" There was an evil grin on Henry's face. He was enjoying this.

"Absolutely. I am good with that," John told him.

"I always wanted to be somebody's worst nightmare," Henry commented.

"You've always been my worst nightmare," his android grumbled.

"You are not a 'somebody,'" Henry fired right back under his breath.

John shook his head. "Okay, whatever, let's make that happen. Send your purchase orders up to Mariah. She is our best negotiator. If I walk out and look over your shoulder, it will only be out of curiosity. I always hated when other people tried to micromanage me, so I sure won't do that to you. On the other hand, if you would like some help, please do not hesitate to ask. You have the ball on this one. Please start with Barbie's ship. I use her ship myself every now and then."

That went a long way toward making Henry feel a lot better about his place in the bigger scheme of things. He finally had a real damned engineering project to sink his teeth into, and the Captain trusted him with the whole job.

While Henry worked on that, John ordered a large steel building for the property. The building came two weeks later on several large android flatbeds. Construction droids were on yet another automated transport. An android crane showed up next, and the process began. Concrete was poured one day and would be ready to build on the next day. While the concrete cured, the android crew unpacked and began assembly of the structure on the ground. The androids moved the construction relentlessly forward, taking no breaks.

By the time John had finished his breakfast on the second day, the crane had begun to move the pieces into place. By noon the following day, they had his building finished, complete with its own outworld steam-fired boiler for heat and power. He inspected his new 20 by 40-meter building with the head android before giving his thumbprint on the android's tablet to approve the final payment.

There had been too many things accumulating on the property and nowhere to put them. Well, now there was. With the LZ taking the place of the trusty little flatbed, it was no longer needed on board the Tesseract. So, John gave the trusty little flatbed a new home in his new steel building. He saw to making a proper workshop in his new steel building, too. It was a nice private place to get away from everything and everybody. He found that making a lot of noise generally kept the curious away. He also loved burning wood in the boiler. It smelled like a pleasant memory. It sounded like one too when he fired up its steam turbine-powered generator.

~~~

Henry had just cleaned up the last tasks on that huge starship project almost two months to the day after it began when a guy walked into the Pig and Whistle and asked at the bar where he might find the crew of the Tesseract.

This time, no one fell face down onto the table full of blaster holes or ruined John's Reuben sandwich. John actually finished that Reuben while they talked. The owner was so glad there was no running gun battle this time that he bought everybody a free round of drinks. He did post an armed lookout at the front door, however. He was not about to take any chances.

"Hello," the man introduced himself to John, Mariah, and Kip. "I am Jim Aronsen of Life Science Systems, right here on Panara-5. We make compact medical systems: basically, a Medlab in a small patient table. They are ideal for small settlements that can't afford a full-sized Medlab. The problem is getting them to the customer. That's why I need you."

"You want us to carry them as freight?" Mariah asked just to be clear.

"Yes, that is exactly right," Jim agreed with a smile. "I have four units ready to go to customers, but I need a freight carrier to get them there."

"If regular freighters won't get them there, then where are these units going?" Kip asked him.
~~~

"WXR3702-3, Suntori-5, Kapton-4, and Renselar-7," Jim answered.

"Oh, I see," John replied. "You are right. Regular freighters don't go to those worlds."

"I will need to go along myself to provide each customer with training," Jim added.

"How long will you need at each stop?" John asked him.

"I would think that one day or so at each place should be sufficient," Jim ventured to say.

John called Jessica over the network, [Jessica, I need you to plot us a best course to these worlds: WXR3702-3, Suntori-5, Kapton-4, and Renselar-7. How many days will that take with a two-day layover at each stop?] He gave Jim a little cushion should it take longer than he anticipated.

[Those are some real fringe outworlds,] Jessica warned John and Mariah. [Angel estimates that to be a 20 to 25-day round trip. When are we leaving? Do I get to blow something up this time?]

[Hell, no. No blowing anything up. I will get back to you with when,] Mariah replied.

"My pilot says about a month round trip. I would think 5,000 Union Dollars each for delivery and another 5,000 for your passage would be fair," Mariah ventured. "So, 25,000 Union Dollars total for the trip, payable half down and half when we return."

Jim didn't even haggle her down. "Agreed! When can we leave?"

"When can you get your cargo delivered to my ship?" John asked.

"Today, if that works for you."

"That would be fine, but I will have to provision for my ship for a month," Mariah told him. "That will take me most of tomorrow. We can leave tomorrow evening."

"Okay, then," Jim got up to go. "I will see you later today with the cargo and your down payment." He shook hands all around and left.

The entire staff of the Pig and Whistle was beyond relieved as John, Mariah, and Kip got up and calmly left. The staff all silently clapped in celebration. It was a spooky thing.

~

Jim's shiny blue Aster showed up at the ship later, as promised. He even brought three extra Mini-Medlabs in the hopes of possibly selling them. Henry saw to securing his cargo while Jim carried the hard cash down payment to Mariah. Henry endlessly grexed at his android the whole time, but in a strange way, that was just Henry Merritt. After that, he went about checking fuel, reactors, and engines on all of the ships for any signs of trouble.

John found himself strangely aloof from all of the hectic activity for the first time ever. He normally saw to the course, but Jessica and Angel did that now. He normally saw to checking the engines and reactors on all of the ships, but Henry saw to that now. Jane saw to household and provisioning with Mariah's help. All of the details were now being handled by his crew.

How strange that felt -- his crew. He briefly recalled that first day aboard the Tesseract and the loneliness. That seemed like a million years ago now, in another lifetime far, far away. His crew. It was a good feeling, like the feeling that the Tesseract was his home now, like the feeling that he had a family now, like the feeling that his life had a purpose now.

Preparation for a long voyage was indeed hectic. The next morning, Jane came along with the ladies on the shopping trip herself, giving the vendors no relief between her picking out only their best and Mariah haggling down their price. But alas, there would be no time for incidental shopping, sadly. Mariah, Jessica, and the girls passed their favorite shops by with only wistful glances.

His bags in hand, Jim came along at 16:00 Zulu as he was told. John had Jim park his Aster in the new steel building for safekeeping while Jim was gone, but that did not stop Mariah and Jessica from coming out to ogle Jim's almost new shiny blue transport.

"See," Mariah just had to jab John, "this is what normal people drive."

"Like I keep saying," John reminded her, "we are not normal people."

"I never accused *you* of being normal," she quipped right back.

"I thought you liked our shiny black Aster Limo," John spun the LZ in a favorable light.

"Actually, I do," she admitted. "Does that make me as abnormal as you? No, it does not."

I am not the crazy one here, John reminded himself as Mariah and Jessica hustled back to the ship. Jim followed John back to the Tesseract, where he was quickly engulfed in the preflight preparations going on feverishly all around him. He stood there on the gangway, just taking it all in for a minute until Henry spotted him and pointed him up to the mess to find Jane. Jane took him from there to his cabin on B-Deck.

"Dinner is promptly at 17:30," she informed him.

"17:30, you say? Okay," he said, looking somewhat confused by that.

"The Captain, he is an outworlder, so he would prefer 17:00. The Missus, she is a proper pilgrim and would prefer 18:00," Jane explained to the very pleasant-looking younger man.

"Oh! I see now," he said, finally understanding that the odd dinnertime was a compromise. Jim continued to unpack and hang clothes in eager anticipation of this voyage.

At the same time, Henry wandered now from ship to ship amongst the M-4s to see if any of them needed any last-minute engineering help.

"Fraking Merc ships," he grumbled to the android. "All built by the lowest bidder… Well, wasn't that obvious? Anyway, we have them up to our standards now… for the most part… well, the important parts anyway. Come on! Move along! Stop dawdling. The Captain says that Barbie is special. She needs extra help, so we are going to go check out her ship for ourselves. Hey! Don't go in there. I said we are headed for Barbie's ship. What the Hell are you thinking? Oh, yeah. You're the android, so I do all of the thinking. Come on."

Barbie was there with a big smile to greet Henry as he came to her ship. Henry made a very thorough and careful check of all of her ship's systems himself, not trusting Barbie to one small bit of it. He found that she followed his every command with a smile. She listened attentively to his incessant ranting, so instead, he turned to explaining to her what he was doing. That was nice. She wasn't making demands of him, or endlessly babbling on, or asking a million dumb questions. That was nice too. After that, Henry rather favored Barbie himself, too, if the truth be known.

"You are a pleasure to work with," he told her as he was leaving. That got him a big smile and a kiss on the cheek goodbye. He left her ship with a smile on his face. Oh, he was still grexing at the android. What did you expect? He was still Henry… or Hack… or whatever the hell people called him.

~

The Tesseract fleet lifted off promptly at 17:00 and made way for open space. It was truly a sight to behold. In fact, Jessica put up the front and rear camera views for everyone to watch in the lounge and mess. The camera views were also available on the whole wall 3D displays in all of the rooms. Jim sat in the lounge in utter awe. He thought only the Tesseract was going on this voyage. He had no clue this was about to happen. He was duly impressed.

Dinner that evening was one of Jane's finest. There was turkey and dressing and mashed potatoes. Jane's android brought it all out to the table on platters and in bowls. Family-style dinners felt warm and homey. Jane joined them and had her android do all of the running back-and-forth. Jessica left Angel in charge of the piloting, so she could enjoy dinner too. She sat next to Hack but insisted on calling him by his proper name, Henry. That made Henry smile.

Sophie already knew what Henry liked, taste-wise. She would give this new guy, Jim, some time before she would find out what his tastes were.

"So, Jim, what got you into this business making small Medlabs?" Mariah asked him.

"I call them Mini-Medlabs," he informed her. "I went to school to become a doctor, but then the war broke out. During the war, while I served as a medic, I completed the requirements to become a doctor. I really like helping people. The people on all of the pilgrim worlds already have big medical facilities to care for them, but full-sized Medlabs are few and far between in the outworlds. What was needed was a more compact version that even small colonies can afford. I don't make a lot of money with these, but they should help a lot of people. That's really what this is all about – helping people."

"That is exactly what we are all about, too," Mariah responded. "Making a difference starts with me. That is our motto. You are just coming at it from a different direction."

"Yes, I am. I like that -- making a difference starts with me," Jim decided.

~

The whole time since Henry was restored, he was concerned about just how much real engineering he would be doing. After all, he reasoned, he was a highly credentialed engineer.

"I am much more highly qualified as an engineer than the Captain is," he complained to Jessica. "I am confused. He gave me the M-4 project and let me run with it. He even said what a fine job I did, but then he has these eight lasers sitting here. Eight lasers, eight engines, he is obviously going to modify the Tesseract's engines, but he hasn't said a word about it to me. After all, I am the ship's engineer. I just don't know what to think."

"Let me ask him," Jessica offered. "I will find out."

Jessica found the Captain sitting at his workstation on the bridge working on, of all things, an engineering problem. Now was the time to speak up.

"Captain, I see you working so hard on your new project, but you have Henry to help you with that. He is really a very good starship engineer, you know."

"Yes, I keep forgetting that… I really should ask him to help me… but my head is stuck on the old image that I have of him as the android."

"I really don't understand what your problem is," Jessica told him. "Henry is the human. Andy is the android. And where you got 'Hack' from, I haven't a clue."

Where would John even begin to explain all of this to her when she didn't even remember being artificial herself? So, he didn't. "It's just me. I am still struggling with it."

"Maybe it would help if you stopped calling him Hack and started calling him by his real name -- Henry. I know he would like that."

"You know, you are right. I need to call him by his proper name."

Even though John really did know that he was the only sane one here, he marched himself down to the equipment bay to find Henry. He walked right up to him and said, "Henry, I have an engineering problem, and I really could use your help."

Well, you could have bowled Henry over with a feather. It took him a couple seconds to even speak, which we know was seriously out of character for the real Henry Merritt.

"Why, of course, I will be glad to help you. What have you got?"

So, John spread out a bold new approach to faster-than-light travel. Instead of making huge long single jumps through time-space, John proposed to make an immense number of very short jumps. The new method would move the ship through time-space harmonically, just like a quantum particle.

"I need to modulate the time-space field coils with powerful ultraviolet lasers to accomplish that," John told Henry. John went to the wall display and called up the eleven-dimensional equations for what he was proposing. Henry took a good long look at them. He hm'ed and scratched his head. He spoke to himself silently,… well, mostly silently.

"My goodness, I have never seen the equations broken up like this before… but this does make each piece small enough to understand. Hm. I can't find anything wrong with the math or the logic. Hm," Henry continued looking them over, mumbling to himself the whole time. John held his peace the whole time until Henry finally got that 'aha' moment.

"Oh, my! Well, I see now, ah, yes, that will definitely create 889.328×10^{12} micro timequakes per second, but only if you can inject the fields almost perfectly in-phase."

"So now you see my problem," John confided in him. "I am not exactly sure of the most reliable way to get that to happen. That's where I need your help."

John was pretty sure that he had his old buddy back. "And I need you to keep this just between you and me. If it does work as I believe, it will be the next leap forward in space travel for mankind."

Henry gave him a good solid handshake on it. "You can count on me, Captain."

And so, the quest to move beyond the tesseract began. John knew damned well that it would work. The Codex files laid it all out theoretically but did not give him any of the physical details to actually build it. That was the test now before John.

John went back to his seat on the bridge and was barely comfortable when Jessica could no longer stand the suspense and asked, "Well?"

"You were right. I have my old buddy back under a new name. I just have to remember to call him Henry, and I really could use the help, too."

Jessica hugged him.

John sent Henry some drawings to show him what he was thinking on the project. When Henry had some time, he marked them up with some of his own ideas and sent them back. They sent the drawings back and forth any number of times over the next few days, each working on them when they had some time, each thinking how brilliant the other's ideas were.

Henry began the work with a new respect for John's abilities as an engineer. He was finally a happy member of the crew. That was how Jessica found him working on the project when she had some free time. Henry, of course, was grexing at the android as he carried an ultraviolet laser for installation. Jessica just smiled and watched for a while.

"Jessica, love, what brings you down here?" he asked when he discovered her standing right behind him, just smiling.

"You, of course, silly," she hugged him hello.

"What, no kiss?" he asked just ahead of getting his socks rocked by a totally loaded kiss.

"Well, now that's what I call a kiss," he had to admit. "But we better get a room for what I have in mind," he whispered in her ear. "Andy, put the laser down and take a break until I get back." The android put the laser down, went to the corner, and went on standby. Henry and Jessica went to Henry's cabin on B-Deck rather than have people see them going to hers on

A-Deck.

Later, John went down to the equipment bay, intending to see how Henry was doing on their project, only to find one of the lasers on the floor and the android in the corner on standby. The android woke up when John entered.

"Where is Henry?" John asked the android.

"Henry and Jessica went on break," the android informed him.

"Hm. They weren't in the mess when I passed," John mumbled to himself.

"They are in Henry's cabin," the android blew them in.

That brought a smile to John's face. "Good for them," he said, but then he wondered if the android was just getting back at Henry for his incessant grexing. The android definitely had an attitude. At first, he was sure that was just Henry. But then he considered that Henry had resided in the android for quite some time. Might some of Henry's ornery personality have rubbed off on the android? Now that was a scary thought.

This is a crazy ship, John thought to himself as he went back to the bridge. *Henry is as strange as it gets. Mariah is yet another prime example of a crazy person in disguise. Jessica isn't far behind Mariah. Now I am even questioning the sanity of the androids, so I guess that leaves only me... and maybe Angel. Okay, Jane is maybe saner than I am. Nah!*

Chapter Eight
Serendipity do.

The end of the Corporate War proved itself to be an equal opportunity chaos creator for both Merc and Union alike. None of the veterans on either side of the conflict had any use for the other, but nonetheless, they were forced to coexist on many of the far outworlds. Such was the case with WXR3702-3. Union farms and families had already begun to settle this world when the Merc families started arriving. In typical Merc fashion, they set themselves up in communes. Despite their past differences, everyone got along just fine, but each to his own. It wasn't as if they were great friends or anything at all like that.

The Tesseract fleet approached WXR3702-3, looking for any signs of approach control but found none. Much to John's surprise, he was confronted by a wing of five surplus Echo-3Cs. "Please state your intentions," their lead ship demanded.

"I can't tell you how happy I am to see you defend your own world. I am Commodore John Korbin. My small fleet has come to bring you some much-needed medical equipment."

"Commodore Korbin, I recognize you now, but what are those mercenary M-3s doing in your group?" he stuck to his defensive posture and questioned everything.

"They are captured ships. You will see them flying Union colors and Union registrations in their transponder returns." John waited while the leader pinged all of his ships and looked them up in the Union Fleet Ship Registry himself.

"Yes, I see. Well, fine then," the leader relented. "How many ships will you be landing?"

"Only one, for now, the Tesseract," John told him.

"Are you bringing the Mini-Medlab?" the leader asked.

"Yes. That is exactly what we are here for."

"Okay, then. Land at these coordinates…" He sent them over.

The Tesseract landed in front of a large community building. There were a number of folks all there to meet them, standing back by the building. The front gangway went down, and Jim ventured out to meet the people. It was midday, and the sky was clear, but there was a nip in the air as local fall was quickly approaching.

Henry had his android carry out one of the crated Mini-Medlabs. They followed Jim into the building. Henry was mumbling things to the android under his breath the whole way. When they got to the new medical room, Henry had his android carefully uncrate the Mini-Medlab as Jim spoke to the medics he was training.

Henry wasn't really listening to any of that. He intended to get this thing uncrated and go back to the ship, but another conversation drew his attention. In the next room over, two men were having a disagreement over what was wrong with their android tractor. You cannot dangle a technical problem like that in front of a real dyed-in-the-wool engineer and not expect him to get involved. Henry introduced himself and went for a looksee at that tractor in the ag building just next door.

Henry found a loose power cable. He easily fixed that, but then he found the next problem.

"You had a loose power cable, but when it came loose, it scrambled the android's memory," Henry informed them.

"Oh, crap. How are we going to fix that?" Hans asked his friend, Jacob.

"I sure don't know anybody who fixes androids," Jacob replied.

"Let me call our Science Officer and see if she can help you," Henry offered.

A half-hour later, Mariah came over to the tractor, her work tablet in hand. Henry had her all set up with the computer access panels open. Jacob and Hans talked to her while she worked.

"It's the only tractor like it," Hans told her proudly. "I own it, but everybody wants to use it. Some can pay, but some can't. I try to work it out as best I can. After all, we Union folks have to stick together. Those damn Mercs all have huge communes. I swear they are going to drive us all out of business."

Henry was right; the android's memory was corrupt. Mariah had to reload its AI program. While that was happening, she suggested, "Why don't you farmers start a cooperative to help you compete?"

"We are not Mercs. We don't want to live in communes," Hans told her.

"No, that is not how a cooperative works. With a cooperative, you all have your own farms and run them as you see fit, but you let the cooperative do for you what it does best."

"Really? What does the cooperative do then?"

"It can help you share your tractor fairly and make sure that everyone shares the cost of running it and fixing it."

"Now that would be good," Hans decided.

"Yeah, but we still have to deal with those damned Merc communes. They pit us one against the other to beat us down on our crop prices but then make us pay top dollar for their wheat," Jacob complained. "I heard they will not sell us wheat this year, only their refined flour – at yet another premium price. See, this just keeps getting worse."

"That's where the cooperative comes in once more. You get your top negotiator to get one fair price for all of your crops. All the farms sell their goods through the co-op and everyone benefits. Everyone gets a fair price, and everyone sells their crops. You could also have the cooperative negotiate a better price on their flour by getting a volume discount. Then everyone would buy it through the cooperative."

"But we don't want any big corporations to take us over," Jacob voiced his concern.

"No, the cooperative is not a big corporation owned by someone else. The cooperative is owned by its members. Every member gets a say. Every member earns a fair share of the profits," she told Jacob, but she could see that he was really thinking about it.

"You know, my husband is always telling me to adapt, improvise, and overcome. That is how outworlders survive."

"Your husband is right," Jacob agreed, nodding his head.

"I see this whole cooperative thing as being just another way to adapt to competition with the Merc communes," she suggested.

"Hm. You might just be right," Jacob agreed.

That was a nice conversation that Mariah thought was maybe the end of it, but later that evening, a delegation appeared at the bottom of the gangway to talk to Mariah. She invited them in, and the meeting took over the mess. It was a friendly group, but everyone had their own opinions. Mariah called up several legal arrangements for their new cooperative as examples until they found one they all liked. A vote was taken, and the first Union co-op on WXR3702-3 was formed.

While Mariah met with her group of people, John met with the local veterans' reserve in the Five Moon's lounge. That was after every one of them had to see the wall with all of his metals, awards, and degrees. Mariah was right; the veterans really did enjoy seeing them.

"These are dangerous skies," Jerrod, the squad leader, warned John. "We are constantly seeing patrols of Merc M-3s. You had us totally spooked when we first saw your M-3s."

"I saw nothing all the way here," John commented. "Let me check my charts." He called up his revised star charts with all of Ishmael's data on them now. Sure enough, beyond WXR3702-3 was a hidden Merc world that did not show up on the Union charts. Even though WXR3702-3 was not on any of the main Merc spaceways, it was still close enough for them to surveil it on a regular basis. John put that information up on the wall 3D display for the veterans to see.

"Here is your problem," John showed them. "You are right to keep your vigilance."

The veterans left later that evening wondering what to do. John wondered too, but his time here was short. Jim would finish his training for these people tomorrow. They would be leaving shortly after that. John went to bed with their situation spinning in his mind.

~

In the middle of the night, Barbie suddenly started hearing Merc traffic on her old Merc quantum-com. Barbie worried that something bad was happening, but she didn't know what to do about it. She materialized onto the bridge of the Tesseract.

"Angel?" She called out when she found no one there.

Angel materialized into the copilot's seat. "Hi, Barb. What's up?"

"I suddenly started hearing a lot of Merc traffic on my old Merc com. It sounds to me like they could be headed this way. I don't know what to do, and the Captain is sleeping, so I can't just ask him."

"You did the right thing to bring this to me," Angel told her. Angel had heard Jessica call Barbie a ditz too many times. Unlike Jessica, Angel saw Barbie always trying to do a good job.

"Can you show me?" she asked Barbie. Barbie played her back the traffic.

"We had better wake up the Captain," Angel quickly decided.

John walked onto the bridge five minutes later, with his eyes at half-mast. He found Barbie and Angle waiting for him. Angel helped Barbie arrange her data visually so that he could see more clearly the pattern that she and Barbie saw naturally.

"Barb saw a familiar pattern in the Merc com traffic that I thought you should know about right away," Angel told him.

"It sounds to me just like ships moving in stages as though maneuvering into a battle zone," Barbie explained to him while Angel showed John the traffic itself on his display.

John turned to Angel to tell her, "I am so glad that we found you."

Angel smiled. "Thank you."

"Please sound the Red Alert, Battle Stations."

Rachel, on Kip's ship, responded right away, "I am waking him up!"

"Thank you, Barb. You did the right thing. You had better get back to your ship now," John told her.

Barbie popped out.

"Make orbit as quickly as you can make it happen," John told Angel. She buttoned up the ship and lifted off into the night while John called

Jerrod to sound the alert. They were almost into orbit by the time Mariah and Jessica came to the bridge in their robes.

Kip formed up with the M-4s into a battle group, waiting the fifteen minutes it would take the Tesseract to join them. In the distance, on the planet below, he could see the local Echo-3Cs also making for orbit.

"They made their first jump toward us," Barbie reported to the group.

"How many ships?" Kip asked Barbie.

"I see com traffic from two warbirds and ten fighters," she responded. Merc warbird-class ships were about the size of frigate-class Union vessels – 140 meters long or so.

"That is hardly a fair fight," Kip commented, knowing full well the superiority of the Tesseract Fleet.

The Tesseract formed up with the rest of the ships and headed out for a confrontation, the five local reserve Echo-3C fighters close behind. They were just as happy to see the Tesseract Fleet take the point. Two more jumps brought all of the parties face-to-face.

John hailed them, "Merc ships, what are your intentions?"

There was a noticeable delay. "Our only purpose here is to defend our colonists on this world. Union ships, we ask the same of you."

"Then we have no quarrel," John told the man he saw in his 3D display.

"Merc colonists on this world tell me that you brought medical equipment here. Is that for the Union colonists only?" the man asked John.

"The Union colonists purchased a Mini-Medlab that we are here to deliver. They have just recently formed a cooperative. If they want to use the new Mini-Medlab, then the Merc colonists will need to negotiate the details of how they will share in the costs," Mariah told him.

"That seems fair," the man decided. "I will wait right here until I hear from my people that is done."

"You do realize that down there dirtside it is the middle of the night?" Mariah asked him.

"We will all be patient, then," the man told them as his image dissolved.

"Well, there you go," Kip now piped in. "Here we sit face-to-face until they all figure out how to share the Medlab we just delivered?"

"I guess we do," John concluded. "Mariah love, you are up. Go use my office and see if you can get the ball moving on this, please."

Mariah was not at all happy in the least. First, these people had the unmitigated gall to disturb her perfectly fine sexy dreams, and now she would have to spend endless hours holding people's hands trying to get a sharing agreement out of them. Jane's android brought her tea and oatmeal to the Captain's Office while Mariah got some other sleepy people down dirtside up at an early hour to work this all out.

~~~

Aboard the Merc warbird Tobruk, the Information Officer got a hit on 'John Korbin' from his picture off of the main display. It was an all-ships alert from High Commander Sarsen Tabbot herself. Captain Shinzai read the whole report, examining the pictures and video carefully himself. This would require some careful consideration.

"Contact Mattock on the planet. I want updates on how this negotiation is going."

~

Almost twelve hours later, Mattock called him back, "Captain Shinzai, I assure you. We have come to an acceptable agreement. One of the options they offered was to sell us a medical unit of our own. We have accepted that offer."

"But the captain of this ship, the Tesseract, is he a deceitful man? Can he be trusted?"

"The Union people tell me that he is an honorable man and so is his crew. Let them land. Let's see if they make good on selling us one of their medical labs."

"So, it will be then," Shinzai decided. It would be a test of this John Korbin's honesty.

~~~

Captain Shinzai appeared once more in John's main bridge display. "Yes, Captain?" John asked.

"You claim to have no quarrel with Mercs, yet you tried to kill our High Commander Sarsen Tabbot."

"Yes, I did. But that is a personal matter, just between me and her and no one else. I swear that if she ever crosses my path again, I will not fail to kill her. You can tell her that I said so. But the war is over. No other Merc needs to fear me. No more people have to die, not Union and not Merc. I have no quarrel with any but Sarsen Tabbot herself."

A smile crossed Captain Shinzai's face. He knew as a matter of fact that Sarsen Tabbot was the most cleaver of all the Merc commanders he had ever known. And, here he was, was face-to-face with the only man that had ever come even close to killing her.

"I will retreat two waypoints," Captain Shinzai told John. "That will allow your ships to return to deliver my people their new medical equipment. When I hear that my people are satisfied, my ships will head for home."

Over the next few minutes, Shinzai's battle group retreated. The Tesseract fleet returned to WXR3702-3, this time with a new set of coordinates, to deliver the Mercs a Mini-Medlab.

"Good grief!" Jim Aronsen said in disbelief. "I wanted to sell more units. I sure hope it gets easier than this."

"Well," Mariah told him, "maybe it will and maybe it won't. At least we didn't have to shoot anybody or blow anything up this time." That drew a strange look from him.

Dealing with the Mercs was simple. They paid exactly the same price as the Union colonists plus shipping. Jim had to show them copies of the paid invoice to prove it. Jim stayed with them and trained their people.

The Mercs were very happy with how well it worked out. Mariah also worked out a mutual aid agreement between the Mercs and the new co-op. Should either Mini-Medlab break down, they would share the remaining unit until the broken one was repaired, or a replacement was found.

~

"Captain Shinzai," John spoke to him as the Tesseract departed two days later, "it seems that the colonists here all get along fairly well. The

Union fighters that you see here are sworn to protect and defend all of the people of this world, not just Union. What are your intentions?"

"We only patrol to keep the peace."

"Then, why not just communicate that to the reserve forces here? That would go a long way towards avoiding misunderstandings."

"Agreed. I will let them know when we are patrolling. We do not want misunderstandings to cause unnecessary trouble."

"I'll tell their leader. I am sure that he'll be happy to hear that."

~~~

Captain Shinzai's Information Officer filed a contact report to Sarsen Tabbot over the quantum-com. At the far reaches of the sector, across the Seven Pillars, she read it personally and looked at the videos herself.

"I knew it! I knew it! The man lives! And yes, he does hate me. And his hatred will make him take chances that he should not. My worthy opponent lives! See, I told you. He even has Union Fleet fooled."

"But Ma'am, he is clear across the sector on some of the farthest outworlds," her XO reminded her.

"Yes, I see that. Redouble the information request. Send it to every outpost, big or small. He works freely with Mercs, so then let him be tracked by his own careless associations. I knew it! The man lives! I will find him, and I will kill him, but this time it will be on my terms.

"But Ma'am, the man is clear across the quadrant, across the full strength of Union Fleet from us," her XO again reminded her.

That sparked in Sarsen a vicious evil thought.

"If I can't go myself, then I will send him certain death. Let us see how he faces his own demise. I will send him a dragon."
~~~

Chapter Nine
The zero point.

Jim Aronsen sat in the mess at lunch, looking somewhat shell-shocked. It was Jessica that first noticed it.

"Are you doing okay, Jim? You look a little dazed," Jessica asked him.

"You know, I heard the comments you all made before the voyage and all, so I kind of expected it to be a little rough around the edges, but this was…." He was searching for words.

"More than you expected?" Jessica filled in for him.

"I thought the war was over. That is what they told us. I thought all of that was behind me, but this was like living a flashback," he told her.

"You are suffering from the illusion of knowledge," John joined the conversation in progress. "Damned lame-ass pilgrim politicians told everyone the war was over. They shouted it from the rooftops until everyone believed them. Everyone was so glad to hear it that they thought it was true, but you just found out up close and personal that it wasn't true then, and it isn't true now. The politicians just assumed that once the mercenary forces surrendered at Zari-Kuut that the war was over. They called in the dogs and pissed on the fire. But it wasn't over, not by a long shot."

"Yes," Jim agreed, "the illusion of knowledge. It sure had me fooled and a lot of other people too, I would bet."

Henry laughed. "Yeah, it sure does, and you ain't seen nothing yet, mate."

"Not to worry, though," Sophie assured him. "My Ka will protect you."

Emma chuckled. "Yeah. He is large and in charge."

"Ka?" Jim asked.

"The Captain," Jessica defined it for Jim. "In Sophie's native language, 'Ka' is the lord high mucky-muck leader or something like that."

"He only thinks he is in charge," Mariah interjected as she entered. "It's my ship, so I am in charge." She said that as if she actually believed it.

"She only thinks that it's her ship," John corrected her. "I hold the ship's title. It's my damned ship. I am the captain, so I am in charge… for whatever good that does me at times. Being the captain of this ship sure does have its challenges."

Jim was still thinking about something. "Called in the dogs and pissed on the fire? I never heard that expression before. Where did that come from?"

"It's a very old saying from Earth," John told him. "My father used to use it all the time. It was from a time in the distant past that Earthmen went out coon hunting. They would set a pack of dogs to hunting a nocturnal coon. The dogs would all be howling and barking. As the hunt went on, the night would get cold, so they built a fire to keep warm. When they shot the coon, the hunt was over, so they called in the dogs and pissed on the fire to put it out."

"It sounds to me like you lived it," Jim commented.

"Actually, I did. My dad used to take my brothers and me out coon hunting. Now, I am sure that what we hunted was not the same animal, but that is what we called it. My dad said that it was like a celebration of our roots."

"It's just amazing how we cling to the old Earth sayings," Jim said quietly.

"It ain't over 'till the fat lady sings," Jessica added her two cents to the ongoing discussion. "I haven't figured that one out yet either, but I will."

"It means that you should never give up, no matter how desperate things seem," John told her. "Like when your team is behind in a game with only minutes left to play, you don't give up. You play your heart out right up to the final whistle."

"What does that have to do with a fat lady?" Jessica asked.

"Apparently, when the game was over, a fat lady would sing," John conjectured.

"Ooh! That puts a scary picture in my head," Jessica decided.

"I guess you had to be there," John agreed.

~

After lunch, John could no longer stand the suspense and just had to see how Henry was coming with his engine modifications. As the engines were built into the ship's spaceframe, he would have to hunt Henry down. He knew he was on the right trail when he saw a pile of cables and tools in the passageway and Henry's feet sticking out of the access tube, its cover removed and set up against the opposite wall.

"Okay! Hand me the cable," Henry called out to his android from inside the tube. "Come on. Farther. Keep feeding it in. Don't stop! What the hell are you doing out there?" he grexed incessantly at the android. The android turned to John, mouthed the words, 'Blah, blah, blah," and made a face.

Dear Lord, these two were made for each other. John was sure now that way too much of Henry's ornery personality had left its mark on the android.

"Captain is here," the android informed Henry.

"I am just curious," John told him in a loud voice so that he would hear. "I didn't want to disturb you."

"This is the last one," Henry called back. "I am just fixing the sync cable to the laser. We will be ready to give this a try in about an hour."

"Great! Let me know when you are ready." John left, shaking his head.

An hour later, the Tesseract fleet stood still long enough for John to test his engine modifications. Jessica took the helm while John and Henry worked on getting all the adjustments adjusted. They were like a couple of kids with a new toy. Jessica had very strict instructions what to do if and when. Kip fidgeted and watched. To his amazement, the Tesseract suddenly faded and disappeared.

[John! John! What the hell are you doing over there?]

[I got it! They are all synced.]

[You got shit. You just faded away! Where the hell are you?]

The Tesseract suddenly reappeared.

[Man, you really had me going there, for a bit. What the hell did you do?]

[It was an experiment,] John explained.

[In what? Disappearing?]

[No, existing as a quantum particle, but we could still communicate over the quantum-com,] John noted. [I wasn't expecting that.]

[But you did expect to disappear, right?] Kip asked just to be clear.

[No. I wasn't expecting that either, but now that I think about it, I should have.]

[Okay, Jess, we can get back underway,] John told her.

John looked at Henry over the intercom display. Henry had an odd expression on his face.

"Now I have to say, you never struck me as the scientist type. I have worked with a lot of scientists, and you are not like any of them. What are we doing? Why are we doing this?" Henry knew full well all of the technical details of 'why' and even that it was a technological leap in engine design. John heard the much deeper 'why' Henry's question was really asking.

"Tactical advantage," John explained to Henry. "Sarsen Tabbot is still out there, and now she wants a piece of me."

"So, is this survival or revenge?" Henry asked him bluntly.

"You know, when she first killed my family, it surely would have been revenge, but I hope I am past that now. My family was not her only victim. Her crimes against humanity are legion. I see this as kind of like a Special Forces thing. I have assigned myself to make her pay for what she has done."

"You are not responsible for doing that," Henry reasoned. "That is a job for Union Fleet."

"Normally, I would agree that well it should be, but you've seen so far they are not capable of getting her. She has beaten them or eluded them at every turn. She is a wickedly cunning witch."

"So, you are going to hunt her down then?" Henry asked him.

"Oh, heavens no. She is hunting me. When I least expect it, she will strike."

"Then this is really a matter of survival," Henry concluded.

"The quantum reality of it is that it is both at the same time," John concluded.

~

Suntory-5 was an amazingly beautiful world but seriously off the beaten path. The Tesseract fleet pulled into the asteroid field around its star to refuel. This was another first for Jim. He sat amazed as the ships entered the tumbling rock zone to begin refueling. Mariah busily identified the asteroids for mining and assigned each one to a ship. Over the next two hours, everyone refueled. John and Kip even made sure to get a few spare barrels of refined fuel set aside. Kip didn't think John was so crazy anymore with this whole barrel thing. While everyone refueled, Jim contacted his customer and got landing coordinates for Jessica.

To everyone's great delight, the Tesseract and Kip landed at the only town on the planet, in an open field on the eastern edge of town, right near the local farmers' market. The front gangway was hardly down when Mariah, Jessica, Jane, and the girls just had to go peruse the local market. Rachel joined them. Jane enjoyed every second of shopping that market for its diverse produce. Jane's mind worked in recipes and ingredients. Each purchase brought them all one step closer to yet another culinary masterpiece. This was why Jane had been chosen by Fleet for this ship in the first place.

Henry had his android set up a couple picnic tables out between the ships for Jane. She wanted to make a nice harvest feast for everyone. John bought a bag of real hardwood charcoal while Henry modified a metal barrel to make a grill. Jane had her android cooking hamburgers and fresh corn on the grill while she brought out bowl after bowl of all kinds of salads and piles of homemade rolls.

The copilots all came across the network to join in the feast. Each of them had a taste of this or that, but overall, ate very little. Everyone talked and enjoyed the beautiful day. John was pleased to see that the ladies had stopped treating Barbie like the family dunce. Barbie still tended to remain quiet and let other people do the talking. In fact, she was a very good listener and didn't miss a thing. Angel sat with Barbie but enjoyed everyone's company.

It was about halfway through his third burger that Barbie finally said quietly to John, "Captain, I have noticed some very strange traffic on the Merc com."

That got his attention. "What do you mean by 'strange'?"

"Little bursts of data that come and go at odd times," she explained.

"Hm. I remember something like that from during the war, but no one ever figured it out," John said between bites. "Good work. Did you save any?"

"Yes, I did."

"Good. Would you please send them to Mariah?"

"Yes, sir… I just did." Barbie smiled at him.

Henry built a nice bonfire as evening set in. A fall chill had everyone bundling up as the night sky filled with stars and the most beautiful view of a nearby nebula that John had ever seen from a planet's surface. Emma and Sophie curled up on his lap under a blanket that Mariah brought out. She snuggled into his side and shared the blanket with the girls.

The flickering fire, the smell of wood burning took John's mind back in time. He could hear his dear mother's words: "What would it profit a man if he gained the entire world but lost his soul?" Back then, he knew what she meant intellectually, but now he knew it to the very core of him. He lived it now, and that changed everything.

This was the soul of him now. His family came first, but his soul was stretched far beyond that. Jessica, Henry, and Jane were now a part of him forever. Kip and Rachel were too, as was Angel and all of his M-4 copilots. For a man that had started his life over totally alone, he was blessed beyond his wildest dreams. But a man who has once lost everything is determined to the very core of him that it will never happen again. So, while his girls fell asleep, John turned his mind to that strange com signal.

~

"None of these folks are medical people at all. I am not exactly sure what to do," Jim explained his dilemma to John and Mariah the next morning.

"How about upgrading the software to a full artificial doctor?" Mariah suggested.

"I wouldn't even know how to begin to do that," Jim admitted.

"I can help you with that," she told him, "but it will take us an extra day to get that done and tested."

"Sure, no problem," John agreed. "This is a very nice place to be stuck an extra day." But John's mind was in overdrive, thinking about Barbie's strange signals. He needed to put his mind to work on a technical problem, so he worked on the engine modification plans for the fighters.

"What is this?" Mariah asked him later that evening when she found him hard at work.

"I am going to need more ultraviolet lasers to modify the fighters," he told her.

"When are you ever going to be done working on all of these ships?"

"When the universe is a perfect place, and mankind lives in harmony."

"Smart ass! Like that will ever happen," she complained.

"A captain's work is never done," he quipped back at her.

"You really do want to get hit, right?"

"I would much prefer to wrestle," he told her with a big smile.

"Yeah, yeah, yeah. I know your wrestling." She smiled back at him. "I am bushed. Come on. Let's go to bed. You can wrestle me to sleep."

"You can wrestle my brains out," he hoped.

~

Their task on Suntory-5 complete, the Tesseract fleet made way. Jim was happy that this customer would be able to use his Mini-Medlab now, no matter how complex a medical condition it faced.

John set a very strange course making mixed use of both Union and Merc waypoints. He spent the whole first day on the bridge, even so much as having his meals brought to him. He was nodding off for brief periods when suddenly the gravity wave alarm went off in his display.

"Red Alert! All ships scatter! All ships scatter!" he commanded. At the same time, he engaged the new laser system to make the Tesseract invisible.

Barbie, bless her little soul, executed the scatter maneuver almost the instant he called it, but Lisa and Ann sat there dumbfounded for several seconds until it sunk in what had happened. Ciara was the second ship out. Then Rachel followed. Finally, Lisa and Ann executed the scatter. That was a definite aw shit.

~~~

The Dark Star captain had seen many maneuvers in his day to avoid him, but this one took the cake. Usually, his sudden appearance would cause confusion, which he would use to his advantage to cut his opponents to shreds while they wondered what just happened. Sometimes, a very alert wing of fighters would all jump out in formation, but this was a first.

A Dark Star's design was diabolically evil. Its Merc designers made it a geodesic sphere to house its multiple sets of engines. Its hull was of stealth materials to make it invisible, impossible for sensors to lock onto. Its weapons were all hidden away in bays, opened only for a few seconds to do their evil. It was the single most lethal spacecraft ever designed. Its only purpose was to stealth attack.

So, what to do? He decided to follow one ship and destroy them one ship at a time. He carefully maneuvered into their jump wakes, which were a jumbled mess. He could only read one clearly. It was from the first ship that jumped out. So, he followed that ship.

~~~

"It's a Dark Star," John said out loud. Jessica was still trying to understand what all just happened. John saw exactly what the Dark Star was doing.

"Barbie, jump to your next waypoint right now!" John commanded. "Jess, jump to her next waypoint!"

When John arrived at Barbie's next waypoint, the Dark Star had already caught up with her. His pulse-cannons were giving her shields a severe pounding. John was not about to play into this Dark Star's strength. Instead, he opened a weapons bay and fired an outworld missile at it. The Dark Star's captain had no idea what was going on. No sensor should be able to lock onto his all but invisible ship, but the missile wasn't using normal sensors. Instead, its throwback outworld designers had it lock onto his engine fields. They were far from invisible.

The missile struck solidly and did take out one of his engines, but the Dark Star had multiple sets of engines. Even so, this was a lot more battle than the Dark Star captain was prepared for, so he quickly jumped out.

"I am so glad to see you," Barbie told them. "My shields were almost at their end."

"Your reflective skin would have saved you, but I am still glad that you're okay," John told her. "I need you to lock fields with me now. We are going to try an experiment."

When she did, John engaged his new laser engine mod.

"Set course for the regroup waypoint," John told Jessica. As she did, both ships moved in a whole new way. They seemed to be flying the course at C35 rather than by making huge, long, separate jumps. Actually, they were making a huge number of very small jumps, but it appeared to them as a smooth linear motion, very much like a motion picture. Jessica just kept cranking up the speed until the indicator read C35.736. Even that hardly heated the engines at all.

To Angel, the harmonic timequake drive felt like she was soaring on a strong wind.

"Wow," Jessica commented. "This is way cool."

"This is what all of my recent engine work was all about," John told her.

"Well, it was sure worth it," Jessica had to admit.

Everyone was waiting for them as they just suddenly appeared at the next waypoint.

"He is still out there," John warned all of the other copilots. "When I call a scatter, you all have to jump out at the same time. Our objective with the scatter maneuver is to create an unreadable jump wake for every ship, so it is imperative that you all jump together."

"When Barbie heard my scatter command, she followed it immediately. Since no one else jumped out at the same time, she left a very readable jump wake. That is how the Dark Star found her so quickly. We have to be prepared to scatter the instant I call it."

John continued, "If you find this Dark Star on your tail after your first jump, then execute your next jump right away. If he stays on your six, then you just keep jumping. Bring him right to the next rendezvous point, where we will all be waiting for him. Whatever you do, do not try to slug it out with this ship. Jump out to your next waypoint and call me."

The Tesseract fleet continued to move down course for the rest of the day.

~~~

The Dark Star captain had no idea how they had managed to hit one of his engines, but they did. His repair androids worked feverishly on it while he used his other engine sets to keep moving. His cleverly designed ship had three sets of engines so that he could pile jumps quickly together without overheating any of them. Left now with only two sets of engines, he was still fully capable of following his prey but much more limited as to his attack strategies.

During the war, the Mercs had dropped tiny buoys into key Union waypoints. The buoys would emit a small, encrypted data packet whenever a Union ship passed by. The problem for the Dark Star captain was that his prey used both Union and Merc waypoints. He just needed to be patient.

~~~

Barbie counted her lucky stars for being saved by her Captain, now even more convinced that she was his favorite copilot. He held her up as an example for her perfect response to his command. It gave her courage as she listened to Jessica recall the incident where the Captain tore a huge piece off of Sarsen's ship. It was like the day she sat next to him as he charged the Merc carrier. The Captain was her model of strength, courage, and cunning.

The Tesseract fleet moved along their course with great caution now, not trusting at all that they had seen the last of that Dark Star.

~~~

The Dark Star's captain was not at all pleased when his head
~~~

maintenance android reported that his engine was not repairable in deep space. He would have to return to a Merc space dock facility to have it replaced, but that would have to wait until later. His patience had paid off. The small fleet of ships that he hunted passed through a central Union waypoint. It gave away their path. He jumped into that waypoint, prepared to finish this quickly, but he arrived too late; they had already moved on. He quickly measured their jump wake and interpolated their current position.

~~~

Barbie noted that mysterious burst data message after they had vacated that last waypoint.

"Captain, I just saw that burst data again," she reported immediately. John quickly looked at his star charts and changed their course. Jessica spread the new course out to all the ships. They all jumped out to the new waypoint as John changed the course one more time to pass back through that first waypoint where Barbie heard the burst message. As they jumped to the next waypoint, Barbie again reported the signal. The light came on for John. He knew how to drive this Dark Star captain crazy now. The fleet circled back to that waypoint, but this time he sat and waited.

~~~

The Dark Star captain was confused. "What the hell is this fleet doing? Are they doubling back?" Then the waypoint buoy reported again. Were they jumping into and out of the damned waypoint for some reason? Then it struck him – who cares why?

The Dark Star jumped into that waypoint, expecting it to be empty, to wait for their return. Instead, he found himself under attack by the whole fleet of ships. They fired on him with rail-gun cannons. His shields were useless against these throwback weapons, so he took a severe pounding before he had to give up and jump back out. But now he was angry and determined to finish this right here, right now.

He returned mere seconds later, almost right on top of the Tesseract. He was about to tear it to shreds when it disappeared right before his very eyes. It didn't jump out. It simply disappeared. He had never seen a ship do anything at all like that. He was dumbfounded.

~~~

All that Barbie saw was that the Dark Star jumped back in -- right on top of her Captain's ship. That evil craft would tear him to shreds! She had to do whatever it took to protect him! She reacted instantly. She charged the Dark Star. John saw what Barbie did but could not react fast enough to stop her.

While the Dark Star was distracted by John's disappearance, Barbie landed her fighter hard on his hull with her landing gear down to cushion the blow. She adjusted her engine fields and jumped out to her 'scatter' waypoint, tearing a ten-meter hole in the Dark Star's hull in the process. The Dark Star jumped out, mortally wounded, gushing out atmosphere and leaving a trail of debris.

"Good Lord! Get to Barbie right away!" John told Jessica.

They found her at her scatter waypoint. Floating next to her ship was that ten-meter section she tore off of the Dark Star when she jumped out.

"Barbie? Are you alright?" John asked her.

"My Captain! You are alright. And you came to find me? I am so happy."

"How is your ship?" John asked her.

"I am afraid my ship's engines are too hot for me to move for a while," she replied.

"I am so relieved that you're fine," John told her, "but I am going to have Henry check your ship over, just the same. I will maneuver over and dock with you."

The rest of the ships jumped in while Henry checked Barbie's ship over.

Barbie appeared on the Tesseract's bridge, came over to John, and gave him a big hug.

"I am so relieved that you are fine," she told him. "When I saw that ship jump close in on you, I was beside myself, afraid for you."

"What made you think to use your jump fields like that?"

"You did. Jessica told us all how you tore a piece off of Sarsen's ship.
~~~

It was all I could think of to do to him."

John hugged her. "You did just fine, but please don't ever do that again. I love you just the way you are – all in one piece. That was a very dangerous move."

"I would follow you to the gates of Hell," she whispered, not intending for anyone to hear.

[Barbie's ship is fine,] Henry reported over the network, [but her engines will take another half-hour or so to cool down enough for us to move on.]

The Tesseract fleet was back underway within the hour. Mariah had run the interpolations when the Dark Star jumped out. Needless to say, John had to find out what happened to him.

They found the Dark Star dead in the water where it had arrived. Jumping out had collapsed its already severely damaged hull. Its atmosphere had all leaked out into space. There could be no survivors from that. A debris field was forming around the wreckage. John sent out a small work-bot. It took pictures close up and some inside the wreck. It took a photo of the ship's ID plate and got a couple of its bulkhead serial numbers.

"Get me Shinzai, please," he requested of Mariah.

Captain Shinzai's face appeared in his main bridge display fifteen minutes later.

"What?" he simply asked John.

John sent him the pictures of the Dark Star's demise.

"Sarsen sent this ship to kill me. I destroyed it."

"You destroyed a Dragon?" Shinzai asked. "I find that difficult to believe."

"Look at the pictures for yourself. If you insist on seeing the ship with your own eyes, then here are its coordinates," John sent them, "but you had better come quickly, or you will find nothing but a debris field by the time you get here."

"Why do you send me this?" Shinzai wanted to know.

"I wanted you to know exactly who was trying to kill who. She was trying to kill me, not the other way around. I wanted you to know that she once more failed to kill me," John told him. "I wanted you to know that this is personal, just between Sarsen and me."

Shinzai looked hard at John. "So, now I know," he said and cut the connection.

"What was that all about?" Mariah asked him.

"Reputation," John answered her simply. "During the war, those Dark Stars were the deadliest craft in space. To the best of my knowledge, we are only the second battle group to have ever killed one, and the first one required a full-sized battle cruiser to do the job. Our brave Barbie did it with just a war surplus Merc M-4."

"But that was a way crazy thing to do," Jessica commented.

"An act of bravery is most often a desperate act committed in a moment of insanity," John commented from his own personal experience.

CHAPTER TEN
Silver spheres.

Jim Aronsen had watched the entire deep-space engagement with that Dark Star play out on all of the 3D displays throughout the ship, on the edge of his seat the whole time. His mind was slowly becoming accustomed to his new view of reality in the outworlds. 'Making a difference starts with me' fits into that picture too, and so did the Tesseract, but right now, Sophie would call this Jim's brain stew. It wasn't a whole, complete thought yet. It was still cooking.

~

John sat on his bridge, thinking like Sarsen. She had an intensely economical method to her madness – maximum impact from a minimum investment. Sending that Dark Star after him was a perfect example of exactly that. To the contrary, Union Fleet always relied on massive overkill. Somewhere between those two extremes lay the perfectly balanced winning strategy.

"So, are we clear now?" Jessica asked into his silence.

"Yes, for now. Sarsen sent one fighter to Aurora with one quantum torpedo to take us out. Then she sent one Dark Star to get us. Both of those failed to kill us… so she is now changing strategies. She adapts to what works and what does not. In many ways, she thinks like an outworlder. Next time we will face multiple threats."

"You say that so calmly," Jessica noted.

"I am a leaf in the wind," John told her. "The leaf exists in a total calm as the storm rages all around it. Fearsome winds drive the leaf this way and that. The leaf flows with winds that are way too powerful for it to resist, and thus it survives. When my mind is quiet, things become very clear, and I exist in the moment. I can ride the winds of the worst hurricane on any planet."

Leaf in the wind? John had Angel's full attention.

"My mind is never quiet," Jess replied.

"Not true," John came back. "When you are flying in battle, your thinking mind shuts down. Everything that you have been trained to do just somehow comes out of you without a single thought. You live in the moment. That is when you are the leaf, flying on hurricane winds."

"I never thought of it like that, but you're right; in battle, time ceases to exist, and I live in each moment," she realized for the first time.

"My father taught me this. He taught me to calm my mind down. I see myself as the leaf and say to myself, 'I am a leaf in the wind.'"

"I will try that," she told him.

Mariah arrived to find the bridge in total silence. At first, she only added to that silence, but you know Mariah. She can't handle silence, not for very long anyway.

"Okay. What's wrong?" she asked, jumping to her first wrong conclusion of the day.

"Nothing is wrong," Jessica barely whispered. "We were just enjoying each other's company."

"With your clothes on?"

"I can fix that," Jessica teased her.

"That does not need fixing," Mariah insisted.

Angel took all of this in quietly. Once, long ago, she was happy being plain vanilla. It was sufficient back then to just do her job and serve. Then Iyo put her to sleep. When Mariah woke her back up, Angel was no longer plain vanilla. Angel didn't know what she was… until now.

Jim came to the bridge to find Mariah. "I think it's time I contacted the colonists on Renselar-7 to let them know when to expect us," he told her as he handed her his tablet to get their quantum-com address. Mariah tried the first address but got no response. That prompted her to try three more addresses on the list and then their emergency contact address from the Tesseract's own database, all to no avail.

"I don't know what's wrong," she told Jim. "They are not responding to any calls through any of their quantum-com addresses."

"What do you make of that?" Jim asked.

"That calls for a full caution approach," John interjected. "A whole colony does not just suddenly stop communicating."

John called Kip. "I think we might have a problem on Renselar-7. Jim and Mariah tried once more to raise them on the quantum-com but got nothing. We need to approach on full caution and recon the situation."

"That's what I would do," Kip agreed.

"Renselar-7 is still two days out, so let me think about a recon plan," he told Kip.

"Jim, what did they send you by way of contact coordinates, maps, and such?"

Mariah sent John a link to the tablet. There wasn't much. There was a new global map for Renselar-7 marked with the town where the delivery was to be made, a map of the town, and Jim's contact addresses.

"I would say no choice but to recon the town to see what's up," Kip told him.

"Yep, that's what we need to do," John agreed.

~

Two days later, the Tesseract fleet pulled into synchronous orbit around Renselar-7 just beyond the horizon from the town. Mariah launched her micro-sat for a looksee at the town. Nothing looked out of place, and there appeared to be people moving around down there.

Mariah next checked into the local planetary network via laser-com.

"Laser-com is up, but nobody is responding," she reported to John and Kip.

"Well, that's not good at all," Kip commented.

Then Mariah scanned the micro-sat's terahertz camera around a bit. She found what would normally have looked like heavy foliage, but the terahertz camera saw right through it.

"Aw crap, what is this?" she asked rhetorically.

John looked hard at her display. "Silver spheres. Those are reptilian ships."

"I hate reptilians," Mariah said. She turned her micro-sat cameras back onto the town that sat at the base of some foothills on the edge of a major mountain range and looked once more at the people she saw moving, but this time she cranked up the magnification. Sure enough, they were reptilians with human shirts and hats.

John had to see this for himself. "They are expecting us. They sent those ones out as a decoy for the unwary. This is not going to be easy. Where are the humans?"

"If I light up my scanning sensors, they will spot us for sure," Mariah reminded him.

"You will just have to do your best with passive sensors then," John agreed.

Mariah looked for well over an hour.

"I can't find any," she told John.

"They must have the humans locked up somewhere," John concluded.

"We are going to have to find them the old-fashioned way," Kip concluded next, "with boots on the ground."

"That's exactly what I was thinking," John agreed.

Mariah gave him one of her looks. "You two think this is fun."

"It isn't?" he asked with a big grin.

"Men!" she just huffed under her breath.

"Sounds like fun to me," Jessica agreed with John. Mariah gave them both a look.

"Hell," Jessica commented to herself. "I might even get to blow something up this time."

Kip's fighter docked with the Tesseract. John and Sam carried their recon gear over into Kip's fighter. Mariah was back to her XO duties on the bridge in his absence.

Kip undocked and circled around for a re-entry out of sight from that main town.

"Twenty minutes to dirtside," Rachel reported to Jessica as they began their descent. Rachel worked the engine fields to slow them down while Kip worked the hard shields as an air brake. It all worked together to get them deorbited as quickly as possible. Kip looked ahead for a clearing to land while Rachel flew them right down just ten meters above the hard deck.

Kip spotted a nice clearing tucked into a flat valley in the foothills, less than fifty kilometers from town. Rachel set them down all nice and gentle, coming to a stop under the cover of some huge trees.

Kip, John, and Sam piled out and immediately began to suit up in their recon armor. They pulled three assault bikes out of the fighter's hold, mounted up, and were ready to go five minutes after boots hit the ground. The air temperature was already dropping from a very comfortable 24C daytime high. It was down to 16C and headed for a chilly 10 – 12C. While that was light jacket weather for humans, it was heavy coat weather for reptilians whose body temperature was unregulated. They slowed down meaningfully in the cold. This was not at all a world they should have chosen for habitation, so they had to have other motives to be here at all.

The assault bikes lifted into the night with John on point, Kip to his four o'clock and Sam to his eight o'clock. They followed the trees and natural cover as far as the outskirts of town, where they hid the bikes in a hedgerow. Kip took the point as they moved from cover to cover, with Sam covering their six. There was a foot patrol, but that was it. All the rest of the reptilians had retreated to the warmth of their silver sphere shelters after dark.

[Set your camo to black,] Kip suggested from past experience with reptilians.

[Reptilians have no use at all for humans and certainly, no use at all for cold planets by their own measure,] John was thinking out loud through the network, [so it makes me wonder what they could possibly want here.]

His answer was found in the next building – gold. The settlers had found a very rich supply here on Renselar-7. This was a bold move on the reptilians' part to just move in and take it for themselves.

The recon team worked their way around the town to a much larger building right at the base of one of the hills. They could see light coming from that direction and hear sounds coming from that building. As they approached, they found it was well guarded, and there was yet another foot patrol to boot.

Sam launched a palm-sized, almost silent drone. He flew it above the guards to an open vent up near the metal roof. When it flew into the building, he could see all of the human men huddled together in groups. Sam landed the drone near a man that was sitting up awake.

"Hi," Kip told the man through the drone's tiny external speaker. "Please be very quiet. Tell us what is going on."

"Have you come to bust us out?" the man asked anxiously.

"Yes, but not right now. We are just a recon team. The whole group will land tomorrow night. Why didn't they just take your gold and leave?" Kip asked the man.

"They are forcing the men to work the mine for them. They have no intentions of leaving."

"This group is only the men?"

"Yes, the men and older boys. They are holding the women and children across town in another big metal building that looks like this one. It's the Community Center. You have to find that building. The lizards have it full of explosives and threaten to blow it up if we escape."

"Well, that's not good. Then we will have to go recon that building right now. Look for us tomorrow night. Have the men ready to go about the same time tomorrow night. Just remember, keep this quiet."

"Will do," the man told them.

[Well, you heard the man. We have to find where they have the women and children,] Kip told John as Sam flew the drone out of there. The hunt was on for another large metal building near the center of town.

The Community Center was smack dab in the middle of everything with open access from all sides, but little if any cover. The recon team got as close as they dared, and Sam, once more, launched the drone. Kip flew it up to find the same vents under the eaves. This time, he could see the women and small children inside. He looked to find one woman still awake, walking about. He landed the drone in front of her.

"Hi. Please be very quiet."

"Have you come to rescue us?" she asked in a whisper.

"Yes, but we are just the recon team. We are trying to figure out the safest way to get you all out of there," Kip told her. "We will be coming back tomorrow night with a lot more people. The men told us that the reptilians have this building rigged to blow up. Is that true?"

"Yes. They set our own mining explosives around the building on the outside, but they have guards."

"Yes, we know that. Like I said, we have to figure the best way to do this, but we will," Kip assured her. "Remember, keep this very quiet. Just keep the other women up and ready to move about the same time tomorrow night."

As the recon team headed back to Kip's ship, John called up to Jessica, in orbit, [Jess, I need the Tesseract down here right away.]

[I am breaking orbit now,] Jessica responded.

~

The Tesseract was parked next to Kip's fighter as the recon team arrived. The recon team drove the assault bikes up the gangway and headed for a meeting of everyone in the mess.

"We are severely outnumbered by the reptilians," Kip first told the group.

"And they have the humans split up. They are forcing the men to work the mine at one end of town and holding the women and children in the Community Center at the center of town," John told them all and carefully outlined the challenges of the building being out in the open and it being rigged with explosives. "I am open to ideas."

"I can cut the metal buildings open with the laser cutter," Sam suggested.

"Thermite would be a whole lot faster," Henry suggested. "We can use thermite to quietly burn a large hole in the metal building to get the men out."

"Good thinking," John agreed. "Then we arm the men, but how are we going to get the women and children out of the community center?"

"Henry," Mariah was more thinking out loud than asking. "Your android has a network node and an atomic field projector, right?"

"Yes," Henry confirmed. "Andy sure does," Henry affirmed.

"Can you train Barbie to disarm the explosives?"

"Sure. She does an excellent job of doing whatever you show her."

"Okay, then. We fly the LZ over top of the building. Then we lower Andy into place. He finds the explosives. Then Barbie materializes and disarms them. It should be as simple as that. If she runs into any problems, you coach her through them via the network."

"That sounds like a plan to me," John decided.

They all had their work cut out for them as daylight overtook them. First, Henry had to teach Jessica how to apply and fire the thermite. Then Henry gave Barbie a crash course on how to disarm civilian mining type detonators. Andy helped Jim load one of his Mini-Medlabs into the LZ. Jim was back to thinking like a field medic. Trying to catch some sleep was nearly impossible, but they all gave it a run anyway.

When he couldn't sleep, John cuddled Mariah, running his hand slowly over her hip.

"Hey! That's not sleeping!" she whispered to him.

"But it sure is relaxing," he suggested. So, she rolled over into his arms, and they relaxed with a passion… so to speak.

Evening twilight began the prep. John had never seen wiry Henry in recon armor before. It looked so ridiculous on him. It took all that John could do to keep from laughing. John grabbed all of the pulse rifles that he had on board as well as their shotguns. Then came the wait for the temperature to drop. It was another beautiful cloudless night, so the temperature dropped quickly below 12° C.

[The reptilians are all inside except for the guards and foot patrols,] Mariah noted from the micro-sat cameras. This op was on. Kip, Sam, and Jessica took assault bikes while John flew Mariah, Henry, and Jim in the LZ. They all flew in formation to the edge of town, where the LZ broke off by flying up high enough to not be spotted. He flew directly over top of the

Community Center building but positioned the rear hatch over the edge so that Andy could be lowered to the ground.

Andy made his way slowly around the building to the first support column, with Henry grexing quietly at him the whole time. Andy flipped Henry the bird the whole time. Henry, watching through Andy's cameras, found the first explosives. Barbie materialized next to Andy.

[Henry, this one doesn't look like anything we practiced,] she told him.

[Give me a second to look it over… oh… yes… Barbie, same as the TEK-4, but the wires are on the bottom. Pull the mechanism slowly up and let me look at it.]

Barbie followed his directions as he slowly walked her through the whole disarm.

[Very good,] Henry finally told her when she had it done. [Good job.] Henry knew how well Barbie responded to a few kind words of encouragement. She had a big smile on her face when she dematerialized.

Henry grexed and grumbled at Andy the whole time Andy searched for the next explosives. Henry couldn't see that Andy was making faces and gestures at him the whole time. This strange repartee continued for six more successful disarms until the reptilian foot patrol decided to stop and sit on the last small keg of explosives.

"We can't wait all night," John decided. "I will have to go down there and handle this myself." Besides, he hadn't hit anybody in quite a long time.

Henry lowered John down. John made his way slowly around the building but almost tripped over something in the dark. It was a piece of steel pipe. He picked it up. Silently he came up behind the two guards and quickly took them both out with that handy piece of pipe. Andy was right behind him. Barbie materialized next to John to finish the last disarm.

As she worked, John heard a loud whisper. He went to investigate. A woman was at the window. She waved to him as he approached.

"There is another bomb inside here," she told him.

Barbie and Andy walked up behind John.

"Barbie, materialize inside the building. This woman will show you where to find the explosives." Barbie popped into the building and followed the woman to the bomb. She sent Henry the video.

"Bloody cold-hearted lizards," Henry cursed them. "It's a cluster frag bomb," he told John.

~

Across town, Kip, Sam, and Jessica made their way to the other building with the men. Jessica did exactly as Henry showed her to apply the thermite to the metal building. She set the igniter and was ready but got no call from John. The seconds ticked away.

[How goes it?] she queried him across the network.

[Not good, but I am working on it. Hold for just a little bit,] he told her.

~

Barbie and four other women carefully picked up the bomb and loaded it onto a library cart. It was a struggle, but they made it to the back door just as John took out the last two guards with that very useful piece of pipe. Barbie dematerialized and reappeared in the LZ to fly it while Henry lowered the cable one more time. John hooked up the bomb to the cable.

Barbie flew the LZ over to the silver spheres -- the reptilian ships -- where Henry carefully lowered that nasty bomb right between them. Henry set it gently on the ground before he opened the release.

"Damned nasty creatures. I hope the nasty beasts detonate the fraking thing," Henry said as Barbie swung them back towards John. "It will serve them right."

[Jess, let 'er rip,] John told her.

~

The thermite wasn't exactly as silent as they had hope for. It also took its own time while it burned its way through the heavy gauge steel of the building, flickering and sputtering.

"Damn," Jessica complained quietly. "This is nowhere near as much fun as blowing something up. Mariah gets to have all the fun."

The flickering light did, however, draw the attention of the foot patrol. Kip and Sam jumped the foot patrol, intending to do this the hard way rather than start shooting, but that didn't work. One reptilian got off a shot just before Sam put him down. Kip gave up struggling with the other one and just shot him.

The thermite completed its task just as Kip heard more trouble on the way. As the men started pouring out of the hole in the building, Sam handed each one of them a weapon until there were no more. The running gun battle started from there.

"What about the women and children?" one man asked Jessica as he exited the hole.

"We disarmed the explosives and got them out," she told him.

The battle became intense for a short while but then let up. Kip regrouped the men and headed around the edge of town. In the distance, a huge explosion went off.

"What was that?" one of the worried men asked. "I thought you said it was all disarmed!"

[Captain, what was that?] Jessica asked him.

[Damned reptilians put a cluster bomb inside the Community Center. We moved it over to their ships. The nasty smart asses just set it off and blew up their own ships.]

Jessica turned to the man. "The reptilian ships."

"Good," was his reply. These men now wanted a piece of these nasty reptilians. "We have a lot more weapons hidden," the man told her. "I am sending some men to get them."

The LZ landed behind John, providing cover as he led the women and children out of town to the cover of the hedgerow. John could see a whole squad of reptilians headed straight for them at a full run. The LZ opened up with its pulse equivalent of the minigun, firing 100 rounds per second. It put that squad in its place, but more reptilians just kept on coming.

Rachel picked up the fight from there. She flew the fighter low, strafing the reptilians, but they were not about to give up so easily and were soon backed up by another whole platoon of reptilian troops. Lisa had dropped out of orbit to back up Rachel, so she joined in the close air support to strafe the reptilians and pin them down. That gave the local men time enough to join up and take positions to defend their families.

"There are a lot more of these damned reptilians here than we counted on," John told Kip privately as the battle raged on.

[Barbie,] John called her. [Please lead the other fighters down to provide more close air support.]

[Yes, sir,] she replied. The rest of the M-4s followed her into the battle.

[Captain,] Angel called him. [She won't arrive for twenty minutes. I could fly close air support until she gets here.]

[Good thinking, Angel!] John replied. [Go for it.]

John was seriously impressed to see Angel fly his ship overhead like a fighter, guns blazing. Neither he nor Jessica had been able to do that, but Angel made it look easy as she took the fight to the reptilians.

What no one had seen was the reptilian squad that had quietly circled around. They suddenly attacked the people gathered behind the LZ. There was a furious exchange of pulse weapon fire that eventually pushed the reptilians back but left Mariah seriously wounded on the ground.

Jim was all over that. He came quickly to field-dress her wound but just as quickly discovered that she really needed immediate medical attention. He pulled his Mini-Medlab out of the LZ and set it up right there on the ground next to Mariah on the live battlefield. He and Henry carefully put Mariah on the table. Normally, Mariah would have been in a total dither and a panic over the Medlab, but she was so dazed and in shock that she didn't realize what was going on.

The battle raged on around them as Jim fired up the Mini-Medlab. It scanned Mariah. At Jim's direction, it went right to work on her just as a pulse round barely missed Jim.

"Hey, asshole! I am a fraking non-combatant!" he yelled at the reptilian, who continued to fire at him anyway. Jim got so pissed off that he picked up Mariah's shotgun and blew that one away.

"Don't you see the fraking white cross on my body armor? Are you fraking blind?" he yelled as he fired the next round at him. The Mini-Medlab took all of twenty minutes fixing Mariah up as Jim stood guard over her, firing at any reptilian within range.

"You're not a bad shot at all for a non-combatant," John complimented him from behind. "How is my girl doing?" he asked, out of breath from running clear across the hot line of fire.

"Just a few more minutes to go," Jim told him. "She will be fine but definitely weak. She will need to rest for a few days."

"We better get her into the LZ as soon as we can," John told him as he and Jim both fired on more reptilians. The Mini-Medlab signaled that it was done with treatment several minutes later, so John quickly scooped Mariah up. When her eyes opened, he gave her a little kiss. As gently as he could manage, he carried her into the LZ while Jim retrieved his Mini-Medlab.

"What happened?" Mariah asked as she became more alert. "You got shot. Jim here put you on his Mini-Medlab and fixed you up."

"And I was okay with that?"

"You were too dazed to question anything."

"You mean, like, why I got shot when I was wearing my personal shield?"

That one had John at a loss, too, so he had to look at her personal shield pack for an answer.

"Maybe it would work a whole lot better if you actually had it turned on."

Then John noticed the tide of the battle had shifted. The remaining reptilians were suddenly on the run. Then he saw that Merc forces had come up on the reptilians' flank.

[Commodore Korbin,] Shinzai called to him through the Merc quantum-com, which Barbie relayed to him through the network, [from the looks of things, you could use our help.]

[Yes, thank you. What brings you to Renselar-7?]

[I got a distress call from the Merc families settled here. Once again, I find you defending both Union and Merc alike. I thought it only fitting that we lend you a hand this time. These reptilians do not like any of us, Union or Merc. They are the worst excuse for an intelligent species.]

[Yes, they are. They shot my wife, but she will recover just fine.]

[I am glad to hear that she will be all right. We have some business here to finish.]

Angel Flew the Tesseract in and landed it crisply right in front of them. She quickly opened the front gangway to pick up the LZ with Mariah, Jessica, Jim, and Henry on board.

[You're clear,] John told her. Reluctantly, Angel buttoned it back up and lifted off.

With them safe, John, Kip, and Sam went out to join up with Shinzai's forces.

~

Two days later, the fighting was over. As things gradually returned to normal, Jim was able to deliver the Mini-Medlab that was ordered by the Renselar Mining Consortium, which was jointly owned by both Union and Merc settlers.

Mariah was getting around, although still not quite her normal pain-in-the-ass self yet. I take that back. She was actually a royal pain-in-the-ass if you asked Jane, who was sick and damned tired of sending her android to wait hand and foot on Mariah.

Jim even managed to get Mariah back onto the Mini-Medlab for another checkup. She was fine with that, although, as Jim found out, she still could not enter the Medlab room on board the Tesseract. That fear was strongly instilled in her by a near-death experience, according to the Medlab scan. It would require multiple treatments for the Mini-Medlab to cure her of that, and so, Jim made sure that she got her first treatment while he had her down.

John and Shinzai spent some time together, just getting to know each other.

"I am sorry that my information officer filed a contact report to Sarsen Tabbot," Shinzai told John quite by surprise. "I did not know what kind of person you really are."

"Thank you. I appreciate that. Like I keep saying, what is between Sarsen Tabbot and me is personal. She killed my whole family."

"Oh, I see," Shinzai replied. "I did not report your killing of the dragon ship, but knowing Sarsen Tabbot, that might not buy you much time."

"Dragon ship?" John asked him.

"Yes. You call them Dark Stars. Our code name for them is 'Dragons.' My crew has given you the title of Dragonslayer."

John laughed. "Dragonslayer? I like that."

Shinzai laughed. "It is true what I have been told about you – you are evil in a good way."

"Yes, I guess maybe I am. So, I will take that as a compliment."

"You are not a freight carrier," Shinzai told John. "You fly war surplus vessels, and you do carry some freight, but that is not what you do. Everywhere I find you, there is trouble."

"You're right. Carrying freight is not what we usually do. Making a difference starts with me," he told Shinzai. "That is what we are all about."

"What do you mean by that?" Shinzai asked him.

"The outworlds are a dangerous place. If we want that to change, then we have to change it ourselves. If we see a wrong, then we have to make it right ourselves. If we see the weak being exploited, then we have to make it right ourselves. We won't stand around with our hands on our asses, waiting for someone else to do it. We will do it ourselves."

Shinzai laughed. "With our hands on our asses! I like that one. Making a difference starts with me too." They shook hands on it.

"I have some Habston lager for you to try."

"I have some Kirinati Ale for you to try."

They both sat and complimented the other's fine beer, thinking all the time that their own was much better. Each man to his own tastes, no matter how different. Two men, once sworn enemies, now finding friendship in the chaos that followed the war, both intent on doing the right things for the right reasons. Both men were trying to make a difference, trying to change everything. Well, they would change what they could.

Chapter Eleven
Big trouble on little Akheron.

It was very odd, to say the least, that Union Fleet would be summoned for a meeting by a Merc world, so Captain Chandrakar of the Union cruiser Star Jammer was going to be as quick to come as the leaders of Akheron had requested. Their Chairman, Malik, was very insistent that Union Fleet come right away. Malik was just as quick to arrange a meeting when they arrived. Captain Chandrakar brought his Fleet Legal Officer with the landing party to ensure that he did not run into any of the same legal nonsense that he got from Al Simmonds on Daggan-7.

Akheron was obviously a modern and well-populated world, even by Union standards, Captain Chandrakar noted as the shuttle made for a landing at its Memphis City Spaceport. To look around at Memphis with its hustle and bustle and traffic, you could be in any large city on Etron or Aurora. For as different as Union and Merc societies considered themselves to be, their common humanity imposed more similarity onto them than either would care to admit.

A proper greeting committee welcomed the Union people cordially when their shuttle door popped open before showing them into the meeting hall in the spaceport where Malik and his team were waiting.

After the introduction, Malik stated the reason for his urgency bluntly.

"Captain Chandrakar, Union Fleet has been attacking and seizing peaceful Merc worlds."

"Chairman Malik, you must be mistaken. The Star Jammer is the only official Union Fleet vessel on this side of the Seven Pillars. We have attacked no one. Our mission here is purely peaceful, scientific exploration."

"This is not true," Malik challenged Captain Chandrakar. "There are ten Union light cruisers in this sector right now. They have already invaded the peaceful Merc worlds of Baratii-4 and Kharon-3."

"I am sorry, sir, but those are not official Union Fleet vessels," Captain Chandrakar tried to explain to Malik. "They are war surplus vessels, purchased by Al Simmonds of Daggan-7 that were supposed to be used as freight carriers."

"What are we to believe but our own eyes? They are indeed Union Fleet vessels, surplus or not. You say Al Simmonds on Daggan-7 purchased them to be used as freighters, but they are still fully armed and carry only troops to invade peaceful Merc worlds. They boldly claim to be operating as Union Fleet! How do you answer that?" Malik challenged what he was being told.

"I can tell you that I have personally challenged Al Simmonds on Daggan-7 over his other such illegal activities under the guise of Union Article-27. This is the first that I have heard that he is attacking peaceful Merc worlds. Please explain that to me."

"On Baratii-4, his light cruisers showed up and filled the skies with landing craft. They first took over Baratii-4's entire infrastructure. Then they started confiscating land and businesses. That is an invasion! They did the same on Kharon-3. Akheron will not be next! Unlike those two worlds, we have a planetary defense system, and we will use it!"

"And I will be right here with you fighting them off if that is what it takes," Captain Chandrakar assured him, "and you have my word on that. Union Fleet does not invade peaceful worlds. I will not stand for Al Simmonds hiding behind the appearance of Union Fleet to do his dirty work."

"How does the Union let this man get away with such an outrage?" Malik wanted to know.

"Back when the Union was first formed, we allowed groups of planets to band together for the common good. We call it 'Article-27.' But when they invoke Article-27, their people have to swear an oath to uphold all of the Union's laws. Al Simmonds has done everything but. The Union was not aware of your plight until this very conference. I will have to go back to my ship to confer with my Admiral as to how I may proceed, but you have my word that I will not allow those ships to invade your world."

"I will hold you to your word!" Malik told him sternly, emphasizing his words with a pointed finger.

The landing party took their leave and made orbit as quickly as possible. The door was closed on Captain Chandrakar's office for the better part of an hour before he called Malik back.

"My first level of response is to order the captains of those ten ships to cease all operations. I will call you back when I have done that."

"Call the other ships, then. Let us see what happens next. I am holding you to your word. Akheron will not be the next world invaded by those ships," Malik insisted before signing off.

Captain Chandrakar took a deep breath and let it out slowly. This was supposed to be a peaceful mission of exploration, not of mediation in a hot war zone.

"Fraking politicians told everybody this war was over," he complained to his XO quietly.

"Then they should be the ones out here having to deal with this mess," his XO suggested.

"Oh, no. They would just frak this up even worse than it already is. Get me the captain of the Aurora!" Captain Chandrakar ordered his com officer. That took her almost another hour to arrange.

All of the captains of Al Simmonds' light cruisers sat for this quantum-com teleconference with Captain Chandrakar. The meeting started out with a full briefing from Captain Chandrakar's Fleet Legal Officer. In it, she cited all of the violations that occurred when they followed Al Simmonds' orders and invaded Baratii-4 and Kharon-3. Despite their protests, in the end, they had to agree that she was right.

She then cited the Article-27section 18 law, requiring their full compliance to Union Fleet Command. By this point, none of them had any intention of arguing with her.

Captain Chandrakar then conferenced in Admiral Erlich himself via the quantum-com.

Admiral Erlich gathered himself up for a stern warning, "You men all took an oath as officers in Union Fleet, so I am only going to say this once, and I want to be very clear. Union Fleet officers take orders only from Union Fleet itself, not some lame-ass politician. Is that perfectly clear?"

"Sir, yes, sir!" the captains all responded.

"From this point forward, any officer or enlisted man serving as Union Fleet who reports any Fleet matters whatsoever to Al Simmonds or his people will be charged with treason. Is that perfectly clear?"

"Sir, yes, sir!" the captains all responded.

"By my order, as of this morning, all of your ships' titles have been recalled by Union Fleet under Article-59. Your ships no longer belong to Al Simmonds or to Simmonds Freightways. I have assigned Captain Chandrakar of the USS Star Jammer as your Captain of the Fleet, in charge of all operations in the Seven Pillars region. If for any reason, you are unable to contact him directly, then you will accept orders only from me or another Union Fleet Admiral as I see fit to put in command. Is that perfectly clear?"

"Sir, yes, sir!" the captains all responded.

"Captain Chandrakar has my own orders to follow. He will brief you." Admiral Erlich saluted the captains and ended his participation in the conference.

"Captains," Captain Chandrakar continued. "I am going to repeat this point for clarity; as of this moment, you are to cut all communications with Al Simmonds, his people, and anyone you know is associated with Al Simmonds. Neither you nor anyone under your command will, in any way, divulge any information on any Fleet operation to any person outside of this command. Am I perfectly clear?"

"Sir, yes, sir!" the captains all responded.

"I am told that your next mission was to take Akheron. Is that correct?"

"Yes, Akheron was set as our next world to liberate," the captain of the Aurora replied.

"Well, as I understand it, that world is perfectly fine just the way it currently is and has asked for our protection. Guess who from." No one voiced an answer.

"Good. Now let's all make a fresh start. You will all make way to Akheron for a face-to-face conference. I am told that Akheron is three days from your current location. I will see you all here in three days." They all saluted, and the quantum-com conference ended.

~

"Chairman Malik," Captain Chandrakar informed him an hour later, "all of the Union light cruiser captains have been put under my command. I am calling them here for a conference on purpose. I was told that, indeed, Akheron was next. All that Al Simmonds will know is that his ships are headed this way. He won't know why. Our successful defense of your world will depend on us keeping this information just between the two of us."

"Then it will come as no surprise when we raise our planetary defenses when those ships arrive," Malik told Chandrakar defiantly.

"Chairman Malik, I would feel exactly the same way you do. By all means, raise whatever defenses you see fit. For now, we need to make Al Simmonds believe that his plan is working."

~~~

However, Sarsen Tabbot was not happy at all. Her crew was also very disturbed over what Al Simmonds had done to Baratii-4 and Kharon-3, but that wasn't bad enough. Now Al Simmonds was threatening Akheron, Sarsen Tabbot's own homeworld. In fact, quite a bit of her crew was also from Akheron, and they were just as unhappy about all of this as she was.

~~~

As expected, Malik raised his planetary defenses as the ten Union light cruisers showed up at his doorstep. He was quite pleasantly surprised to find that each one of the captains called down to greet him and personally assure him of their peaceful intentions. He smiled and accepted their kind words gracefully as he kept his planetary defenses on high alert.

"Chairman Malik," Captain Chandrakar called down to him last. "I would like to propose that I send down to you a shuttle with some of our finest legal officers."

"To what purpose?" Malik demanded of him.

"Their goal would be to sign a treaty between the fine, free people of Akheron and the Union."

"You are demanding our surrender?"

"Oh, no, quite to the contrary. We would like to propose a mutual defense treaty wherein the sovereignty of Akheron will be respected. We would like to propose to come to your defense if you or your sovereignty is in peril. We are offering our friendship."

That took Malik quite by surprise. "That sounds very reasonable. You may send down one unarmed shuttle. We will just see about this." And so, the negotiations began. In good faith, the ten light cruisers backed away from Akheron two full waypoints to indicate their peaceful intentions.

~~~

Sarsen Tabbot carefully arrayed her ships before sending one M-4 fighter ahead to the next waypoint. When that fighter reported the proper all-clear, three more fighters were sent. This was a very careful, deliberate dance, moving an entire battle group. Next, two warbird-class vessels were sent, quickly followed by five light cruisers. It was a slow, laborious task that would have bored Sarsen. Instead, she had her best tactical sub-commander doing all of the work while she supervised and considered battle tactics.

~~~

On Daggan-7, Melissa was scrambling. "What do you mean, you can't get ahold of any of our ships," she asked the Fleet Liaison Officer assigned to the President's staff.

"I mean just that: I can't get ahold of them. They refuse to answer any of my calls."

"Why would they do that?"

"As best I can figure, official Union Fleet protocol is to cut all outside communications while an operation is in progress."

Now Melissa was caught up in the lie -- the lie that the ships were official Union Fleet under Article-27 -- the lie as told by Al Simmonds himself.

"But our ships… our Union light cruisers… have never operated this way, and that has worked perfectly fine until now. This obviously does not work. We need to go back to what works," she tried to reason with Lieutenant Commander Grayson.

"Ma'am, with all due respect, Union Fleet does not operate by your rules or by President Simmonds' rules, even if you think that is what works for you. Union Fleet has its own protocol that must be followed. Apparently, the captains of the ships are just following Fleet protocol, as well they should."

"I have been told that the ships made way for Akheron. Are you telling me that the operation to liberate Akheron is underway?"

"No, Ma'am. I am not allowed to tell you anything about any Fleet operation in progress."

Melisa smiled. In her mind, he just told her that indeed the operation to take Akheron was in progress. That was exactly what she was looking for. Melisa left the Lieutenant Commander standing there as she hustled away to see President Simmonds.

When the door closed behind Melisa, President Simmonds and his closest advisor, Frank, were sitting there waiting for her.

"Well?" President Simmonds asked her.

"The operation to take Akheron is in progress," she reported what she thought was what they were waiting to hear.

"And?" He prompted her further.

"As best that Lieutenant Commander Grayson could figure, the captains are exactly following correct Fleet protocol in ceasing all outside communications while an operation is in progress," she gave him the whole story as she saw it.

"How am I supposed to tell them what to do if they won't communicate with me?" he all but shouted at Melisa. She cowered in place, not knowing what to expect.

He softened his words. "I am not shouting at you, Melisa. I am just upset." She smiled. "Thank you, Melisa. Please leave us to discuss business." She left as quietly as she could.

"Good Lord! Frank! What a Roratanian Cluster Frak we have going on here. First, I find that I can't contact my defense contractor. Now my own ships' captains won't call home. What the frak is going on?"

"Looks to me like we just bought the wind, Boss. My bets are that Sarsen got pissed off about us taking over her damned Merc worlds and is not about to see that happen to Akheron. If you ask me, we got the whole damned war started all over again. This does not sound good."

"Frank, my man, maybe you are right. This isn't going to turn out well no matter who wins."

"Shit, I would be a whole lot more worried if Sarsen Tabbot wins. Then we might be the next world she decides to destroy," Frank conjectured.

"You got that right, Frank, but what do we do now?" Al Simmonds mused.

"We have to warn our fleet that she is coming. We can't let her take them by surprise. That would be a total fraking disaster," Frank offered.

"Exactly. Two-part plan. Part one -- call Lieutenant Commander Grayson in here."

Lieutenant Commander Grayson fully expected the same crap in person that he got from Melisa, so he set himself to be as calm and respectful as he could under the circumstances. Instead, when he arrived, he found a very concerned-looking President Simmonds sitting behind his desk. "Yes, Mister President, how can I serve you?"

"I understand that my ship captains are following fleet protocol, cutting all communication during an operation in progress."

"Yes, sir. That is my current understanding of the situation," Lieutenant Commander Grayson responded.

"Then here is my dilemma: how do I warn them that Sarsen Tabbot's entire battle group is about to attack them?"

"I am not exactly sure," Lieutenant Commander Grayson admitted but was now concerned himself. "They may not be responding to my messages, but I know that I can still *send* them a message. I know they will still see it."

"Well, you damned well better do just that with all due haste,"

President Simmonds told him.

"Yes, sir!" Lieutenant Commander Grayson responded and left in a big hurry.

When Lieutenant Commander Grayson left President Simmonds alone, Frank once more returned. "And now for part two. I am really not looking forward to this."

~~~

Captain Chandrakar was in his conference room, debriefing the negotiating team when President Simmonds' call came in. Captain Chandrakar took the call in his private office.

"Yes, President Simmonds, what can I do for you today?"

"Have you had any contact with my light cruisers in the past week or two?"

"Can't say as I had," Captain Chandrakar replied. "And why would that be?"

"I can no longer seem to raise them on the com."

"I don't see how I can help you with that," Captain Chandrakar addressed that point.

"Well, I sure hope that you have better luck than I do, then. I am afraid that my Merc contractor may be on the way to attack my Union ships."

Despite this distressing bit of news, Captain Chandrakar remained calm. "You do seem to have your problems, as I recall trying to explain that to you at our last encounter. I will not see any Union ship come to harm that I might possibly be able to prevent. I will have to see what my communications staff can do to contact your ships. I had better get to that right away."

"Thank you," President Simmonds told him in closing.

~~~

A single Merc M-4 jumped into Akheron near space to find a lone Union cruiser, the Star Jammer, in synchronous orbit. Sarsen's entire battle group jumped in seconds later. Her own heavy cruiser flanked by five light cruisers. Two warbird-class ships took the point as her entire wing of fighters deployed across the gap that separated her battle group from the

Star Jammer.

"Commander Tabbot! Commander Tabbot!" Malik appeared on her main display.

"I have no time to talk right now, Malik," she told him angrily.

"You will take the time! I am ordering you to stand down!"

"Who are you to order me?!" she snarled back at him.

"Listen to me! Stand down! We have this all worked out. We are about to sign a separate peace treaty with the Union, and you are about to screw that up!"

"You have already surrendered?"

"We have done nothing of the sort! There was no surrender! Akheron remains a free and sovereign Merc world, and this peace treaty guarantees that it will stay that way. It can include you too, but you must stand down."

"What do you propose?" she asked Malik.

"Akheron will sign a treaty of mutual aid. If we are attacked, we may call on them to defend us, and so it will be with Union ships. If they are attacked, they may call on us for our help. 'Our help' is you. Akheron is your homeworld. We have every right to call you 'our defense.'"

"The Union dogs will never agree to that," she replied.

"Like it or not, we will give them no choice. I will demand it as a part of this treaty."

Sarsen was not happy at all but gave the command for her ships to stand down. She never thought for one minute that Malik's demand would ever be met, but she could let those chips fall where they may before she made her move.

~~~

Captain Chandrakar was not happy either with the solution worked out by Malik. He had to confer with Admiral Erlich for Fleet approval of the treaty. He first sent the Admiral advanced copies for Fleet's proper review, so he knew that Admiral Erlich would know his concerns. At the appointed hour, Admiral Erlich appeared on the display in Captain Chandrakar's private office.

"So, Rafti," Admiral Erlich called him by his first name. "What have
~~~

we got here?"

"A compromise at best, but a good compromise for all parties as I see it. We stopped this crazy man on Daggan-7 from starting the whole damned war all over again way the hell out here. On the other hand, I would rather have seen Sarsen Tabbot lined up in front of a firing squad and shot for her war crimes, but I guess that is not going to happen."

"Apparently not," Admiral Erlich had to agree, "but we did get her away from the Seven Pillars and that totally out of control politician, Al Simmonds. By this treaty, she is limited to defending the Merc worlds beyond the Seven Pillars. It specifically excludes the Union world Daggan-7. What do you think she will make of that?"

"Dealing with her up close and personal, I would have to say that she will go back to Baratii-4 and Kharon-3 and summarily hand Al Simmonds his ass."

"She is one tough character," the Admiral agreed. "She will be bound by the treaty to defend Union vessels in her territory. I wouldn't exactly hold my breath waiting for that to happen, but at least she won't be attacking them. The Joint Chiefs all agree; the Union will definitely benefit from this treaty. You are hereby authorized to sign this treaty as the Union's official representative… but make it look good."

~~~

Captain Chandrakar, for all outward appearances, with grave reservations, reluctantly signed the treaty as a duly authorized agent of Union Fleet. Malik was not happy either; Akheron was officially at peace with the Union by his own hand. He could spin that as a moral victory all he wanted, but a lot of other Mercs would not see it that way.

Sarsen Tabbot was the least happy. This treaty closed her universe down to a very small space for her to operate in. It made her a policeman, a mere public servant, not a warrior queen, but this was not the last word for her. Like the Union outworlders that defeated the Merc forces, she would adapt, improvise, and overcome. The best of the worst of her had yet to unfold.

Captain Chandrakar sent the ten Union light cruisers back across the
~~~

Seven Pillars with orders to report to Admiral of the Fleet Suzanne Johnson on Aurora with all due haste. When they reported their crossing of the Devil's Pitchfork, Captain Chandrakar made every reasonable effort to continue with the original scientific exploration mission that brought him out all this way to begin with… That would be after he went to four more Merc worlds to offer them the same peace treaty with the Union that Akheron had signed. He wasn't exactly happy with that. He more fancied himself an explorer than a statesman, but he served as Fleet saw fit to deploy him.

Chapter Twelve

Double, double, toil, and trouble.

John was back at work on those Codex files at his station on the bridge when Mariah came in. She seemed in a bit of a huff. So, what else was new?

Ten minutes into the silence, she said quietly to him, "I don't recall you looking very concerned when you found me wounded on the ground."

"I don't imagine that, lying flat on your back like that, you could have possibly seen the crazy man running across a hot line of battle, dodging pulse rounds the whole way, to get to his wounded wife," John told her quietly, without looking away from his reading.

"You still didn't sound very concerned," she persisted.

"How could I do that to you? Instead, I picked my wife up lovingly from the Medlab with a smile and a kiss. Even though there was a battle raging around us, I carried you as gently as I could into the LZ. I stayed with you as long as I dared."

"Yes, you did," she saw it differently now. She was happy now.

"How much longer to Kapton-4?" she asked Angel.

"Two more days," she responded with a smile.

Mariah sat there at her station, half-watching Angel, half-watching John. *What is it with all of these artificial copilots that has them all drooling over my man?* She asked herself.

But that was not at all what Angel was thinking. At first, Angel had wondered about her new captain. He certainly didn't look anything at all like any captain before him, so she read all of the ship's logs since the crash. She read his service file. It was true; he was like none of her previous captains. He was a man of integrity. He was a warrior in the truest sense. His defense of Panara-5 was brilliant. He was a commodore, not a captain, so even Union Fleet recognized this. He was a man with a righteous cause. Barbie had whispered that she would follow him to the gates of Hell. But most of all, Iyo chose him. In the end, that was all that Angel needed to know.

All the time Mariah was sitting there thinking, John studied those Codex files. Some of the time, he simply read them. Some of the time, he ran the equations through a math processor to see all of the permutations of each individual equation for himself. He was learning this his own way, but it was not like just a simple interest anymore. John was like a man obsessed.

"Why is this so important to you?" she asked him.

He stopped what he was doing and turned to her. "You are most important to me, as are my daughters. I love you all dearly. Jessica, Henry, and Jane are also important to me, as are all of my copilots. Some very nasty people out there want a piece of us. I have to stay one step ahead of them. I need every tactical advantage that I can get to do that… oh yeah, and I have to make sure that you turn on your shield pack."

"Oh," Mariah said, that was the right answer. At least his head was in the right place.

John got up, finally, and went to the ring room, deep in thought. He put his hand on the control panel. It came right up in his Mindlink display. He needed to try something, so he called up the SPACE menu and found QUANTUM PORTAL. You can read the directions for something a hundred times, but it's not like actually doing it. It's like reading a recipe. You can read it a hundred times, but you don't know what it tastes like until you do the cooking.

~

Watching the shimmering wall that formed inside the ring, John pushed the distance reticle out until it passed right through the side of Barbie's ship onto her bridge. It was the weirdest thing, like running a live, full-color x-ray machine. John stepped through the ring, right into Barbie's ship.

[Captain?!] she asked in disbelief.

[Hello, Barbie. I am just visiting.] He kissed her on the cheek, turned around, and disappeared back through that shimmering wall of light as quickly as he came.

Hey, that was way cool, he decided.

~

Kip sat in his mess with a hot cup of java when a shimmering wall of light suddenly appeared. John walked through it.

"Hey Kip, come on with me," John beckoned. He led Kip back through the shimmering wall over to the Tesseract. Kip found himself in the ring room.

"Oh, come on now," Kip said, looking all around. "Where did you hide the smoke and mirrors? This is way weird. Where the hell are we?"

"In another one of those convoluted rooms on the Tesseract," John told him, all excited.

"And what in the blue blazes is that thing?" he asked, pointing at the ring.

"A time-space atomic field coil," John told him.

"Oh, well, that explains everything – NOT."

"It can make quantum portals through time-space. You know – stable wormholes," John explained this time.

"Okay, now that makes sense. Stable wormholes I understand, but I thought that everyone told us that it was impossible to create stable wormholes."

"Well, we just did it. So how impossible could it be?" John asked.

"Not at all, I guess," Kip admitted. "Now that just has to be extremely useful."

"That is exactly what I was thinking," John agreed. "Come on. Let's go sit in the mess, and see how long it takes anyone to notice that you're on board."

"Fat chance of that. I bet Rachel didn't miss one small bit of my leaving with you."

"You're on," John agreed. "Let's go see."

The two of them sauntered into the mess and sat down as if nothing at all was awry.

"Jane, can you please send us a couple fruit juices," John requested.

Jane's android brought the drinks.

"Oh, come on," John complained. "They should be here by now."

~

After John had left Barbie's ship, she called Lisa.

[Captain just came to visit,] she told Lisa.

[Really? But you didn't dock, so how did he do that?] she asked skeptically.

[A shimmering wall of light formed on my ship, Captain stepped out of it and kissed me. Then he left the same way he came.]

Lisa was about to call that a hallucination when Rachel joined the conversation, [Hey, Captain just appeared on my ship. He grabbed my Kip and they left through a wall of light.]

[Where did they go?] Lisa asked.

After a few minutes, Jessica joined the conversation. [I found them on one of my cameras. They are sitting in my mess.]

[What are they doing?] Rachel asked her.

Mariah looked at the camera. "Just look at those two troublemakers sitting there in the mess with big shit-eating grins on their faces, all smug, just waiting for us to go down there and make a big fuss. Well, I, for one, will not. Let them sit there until they rot."

"I thought you told me that all men smelled like that," Jessica teased her.

~

"This is taking way too long," Kip decided after a half-hour had passed. "I think we are busted, and they refuse to play."

"Okay, then let's clam up and see how long they hold out," John whispered to him. They got up and headed back to the ring room. John fired it up and formed a quantum portal to Kip's ship. Kip left as quietly as he came.

~

Kip sat down in his pilot's seat on the bridge of his fighter and just went back to work looking over the navigational notes for their present course as if nothing at all had happened. Rachel looked at him with a 'well?' look on her face, but he didn't say a word. Kip just smiled at her with a puzzled look on his face, and likewise, did not say a word.

~

John went back to his seat on the bridge, and likewise, went back to his Codex files as though nothing at all had just happened… but he had three women to contend with. Angel would have no part of Mariah or Jessica hassling her captain. Jessica gave him the 'well?' look, but Mariah was in one of her typical huffs over this and refused to even look at him.

The silence went on until 17:30, dinner. The bridge crew all came to the mess in silence. Henry and Jane had no idea what was going on when they discovered the silence. Jim came to the table and was also baffled by the silence. Then Sophie and Emma came to the table. Sophie took one look around. She immediately got up, came over to John, put her little hands on her little hips, and asked him, "Ka, what did you do now?"

John couldn't keep a straight face. "I didn't do anything. All I did was to go for a walk over to Barbie's ship and invite Kip over for a drink."

Sophie then went over to Mariah. She crossed her arms on her chest and tapped her foot. "Mom, the ball is in your court. That does not sound so bad to me."

"Oh, yeah? Then ask him what he is trying to make us ask him about," Mariah whispered to Sophie.

"Oh? He isn't telling, so you refuse to ask? Oh, come on, Mom. Isn't that being a bit childish?" Sophie asked her.

Now that really pissed Mariah off, but she never got mad at Sophie. Instead, she threw some mashed potatoes at John. To which he hit her with some gravy. The food fight got hot from there, with all manner of edibles used as weapons. In the end, everyone was laughing. John started dipping his potatoes in the gravy on Mariah's blouse while Jessica picked the peas out of her hair. Henry tried to find the piece of meat that Jessica had put down his pants for no damned reason whatsoever. In the end, they all laughed about it.

The only unhappy person was Jane's android, who would be left to clean this whole mess up. Henry called his android to help. Jane had to call her entire cadre of cleaning bots to this task; they had made such a mess.

Jane served desert herself only after everything had calmed down. "Now, there will be no throwing this!" she scolded them. "It took me way too long to make it for you all not to taste it. Now, be good!"

John could have sworn that he saw Henry's android feel Jane's android's ass when he thought that no one would see him. She slapped his hand away but not very convincingly.

I am not the crazy one here, John repeated to himself.

Jim just calmly ate his dessert. This was definitely a family ship. They were a little rowdy for his tastes, but he enjoyed every second of it. It was refreshingly different from his calm and proper, almost cloistered life until now.

~

Later that evening, as John and Mariah prepared for bed. John crawled naked into bed first. He was expecting Mariah to do the same, but she appeared in a nightgown instead and stood at the foot of the bed.

"Well?" she asked, with hands on hips. "Start talking."

"It will cost you," he told her. "Remove the top ..."

Needless to say, he told her everything... one little bit at a time.

I got everything I wanted, he thought, *and I got hot sex for what I would have told her if she had just asked.*

I got everything I wanted, she thought, *and he told me everything for the hot sex he could have had all along if he had just come clean right at the start.*

They each celebrated their victories with another round.

~

The next morning, John had Mariah, Jessica, Sam, and Henry in the ring room to learn what this was all about. His first objective was to fetch Kip. John fired up the ring and sent its shimmering wall into his ship. Kip walked through with a big smile.

"How nice. You all came to greet me this time," he joked.

"First, I will need each of you to learn how to operate this; so, everyone, gather around," John told them as the demonstration began.

Mariah stepped up first. She always had to be first at everything. John had the control panel identify her. He then commanded, "Mariah, Authorized User."

[Mariah, Authorized User,] it responded.

John repeated this for each of them. He then had each one of them find one of the M-4s to send Sam and retrieve him. This took some patience, but it was necessary.

"Now we all have a good idea what this thing can do," John told them. "Somewhere out there, dark forces are planning our demise. The only thing that might save us could be some very small tactical advantage that we have, and this might be it. I need ideas to use this gadget. If we need to experiment, then let me know so we can do that safely."

"Will it work through shields?" Kip asked.

"We need to try that," John agreed. [Lisa, would you please raise your shields.]

[Is there a problem?] she asked as she put them up.

[No. We are just trying something,] John replied.

"Jessica, can you please send Sam into Lisa's ship," John challenged her.

Jess went right to that, maneuvering the quantum portal with impressive skill. Sure enough, a minute later, she had the quantum portal open into Lisa's ship. Sam went right through, grabbed Lisa, kissed her full on the lips a good one, and then came right back.

"As long as I get to kiss the girls, you can send me anywhere," Sam volunteered.

[Send him back,] Lisa requested. [He'll get a lot more than a kiss next time.]

[You can put your shields down now,] John told Lisa.

[I'll come back later,] Sam promised her.

[I'll leave my motor running until you get here,] she replied.

[Conjugal visits are not what this thing was intended for,] Mariah made her feelings known.

[I might have given you that point some time ago, but I wouldn't be so sure anymore,] John replied, keeping in mind that the anoza had made him picture Jessica's bare backside to access their Codex files until now.

[No matter what the reason, we all can use the practice making quantum portals.]

[Men!] Mariah humphed.

Leave it to Henry, though, for good ideas. "What goes everywhere on a big starship but is invisible?" Henry asked, but no one knew the answer. "Work-bots and androids!" he told them.

Mariah ran with that idea, "We put a network node on a small spider-bot and send it through the quantum portal to spy on them."

Henry added to her idea, "We add a Merc wi-fi adapter to it, so we can spy on them no matter which side they are from."

"Great," John encouraged them. "Henry has the ball on this. He and Mariah will get a spy-bot ready to go and stage it in the ring room. I am putting up a message thread on the ship's bulletin site so anyone with any idea at all can post it and we will see where this goes."

Before John could believe it, the other copilots were requesting 'visits.' All he could do is shake his head and hope that Sam was up to the task… and Mariah didn't find out.

~

Two days out from Kapton-4, Jim contacted his customer. To his great relief, there was nothing at all wrong on Kapton-4. Jim went to the bridge to let the Captain know.

"But I did get a new set of delivery coordinates," Jim told John.

John called up the global display for Kapton-4 from his database, locating both the original and the new delivery coordinates.

"The coordinates are in completely different towns separated by quite a distance. Something sure does not look right to me," John said out loud.

"This doesn't sound right to me either," Jim mused. "I know the guy that made the purchase. The one that answered my call this time was definitely not the one I sold it to."

"I say we do some recon before this gets out of control," John suggested.

"So much for nothing wrong," Jim could only comment with a sigh.

~

Kapton-4 was more than just a perfect Earth-Class planet; it even had a single moon and a tilted pole to make its climate indistinguishable from Earth's… at least according to all of the legends. The original purchaser lived in Metro, a medium-sized metropolis smaller than Habston, in the middle of farm country. York, the new delivery site, was not much bigger, but it was located seaside.

The Tesseract fleet pulled into orbit about mid-day, Metro local time. Jim was not privy to the ring, so Kip docked with the Tesseract to take Jim and John on board for the drop to dirtside. Twenty minutes to land put them right in the middle of town, landing in an open square. Two men came out to greet them.

"Hi," Jim opened up. "I am Doctor James Aronsen. I am looking for Mark Watkins."

"He's inside the Town Hall. Come on this way." One of the men told them. Kip stayed with his fighter. John accompanied Jim to see about this delivery. Town Hall was a relatively new building and very well kept. Mark Watkins came out of his office to greet them.

"Doctor Aronsen, this is a pleasant surprise," Mark told him with a firm handshake. "We were expecting your call but never got it."

"I tried to call, but I got Herman Schwartz instead."

"That rotten piece of crap had the planet's com address changed again!" Mark Watkins went into a tirade at those dirty rotten so-and-sos over in York. This whole feud got started over one pig. Apparently, it got loose from a farm in Metro territory and destroyed the flower garden of a woman in York territory. Damages were demanded and about to be paid until someone from York shot the pig and had a big pig roast, as much as to say, 'up yours!' Then someone from Metro shot the guy that shot the pig. Well, after that, all hell broke loose.

"All that aside, I have your new Mini-Medlab ready for delivery," Jim told him.

"Great! Then let's get the ball rolling," Mark said enthusiastically.

"I will need to land my much larger ship," John entered the conversation.

"Can you fit it into the town square?" Mark asked.

"Sure, but we will have to send the fighter back up into orbit," John told him. "Come on, Jim. Let's get your stuff out of the fighter." Jim gave him a funny look but followed him to the fighter.

"What are we doing?" he asked John when they got back to the fighter.

"These people have some kind of a feud going. The people over in York were trying to hijack this delivery. We scotched that, but maybe we can solve the bigger issue."

"How are we going to do that?" Jim wanted to know.

"Let's just get this delivery done and get you paid," John told him. "We just won't discuss the other folks at York anymore."

"Oh, I see… I think," Jim answered, but he really didn't.

The Tesseract landed in the town square 30 minutes later. The front gangway came down. Henry's android carried out the crated Mini-Medlab for this customer. Henry and Jim went into the town hall for Jim to begin his delivery.

"What's going on?" Mariah wanted to know as she and John sat at the bottom of the gangway enjoying the pleasant spring day happening all around them.

"Jim is delivering a Mini-Medlab to his original customer," John told her.

"What about the second guy? What is going on with that?"

"There is some kind of feud going on here, so I am pretty sure that no matter who gets the Mini-Medlab, they have no intentions of sharing anything."

Mariah thought about that for a second. "But Jim had a contract with these people, so he is delivering it here. Okay. Legally, that works, but that does not solve the feud."

"We don't have the time for that. Hell, the feud may not even be solvable. I have a better idea. After Jim gets done here, we land over at York and act like nothing happened. He was trying to hijack the sale, so we just let him think that he did. Jim can deliver him a Medlab of his own and get paid for that one too."

"Won't they find out that we sold them two?" Mariah asked.

"They have a full-blown feud going on here, so who knows if they will ever figure it out. Even if they eventually do figure it out, we will be long gone by then. In the meantime, each side will have the medical care they need."

Mariah considered that for a second. "Okay, that works for me. There are no legal issues with that approach. Even if I did mediate the feud, who is to say it doesn't flare right back up over some other dumb issue or even the same one."

"That's right. My way, at least we can get this done and just leave," John commented.

"But I will be filing a report to Union Fleet," Mariah continued, "to let them know about the problems here. They will need to know that the guy at York hijacked the com address. You had better find out this town's com address so I can give that to Fleet."

[Henry,] John paged him through the network.

[Yes, Captain?] Henry replied.

[Can you please get us this town's quantum-com address when you get a chance?]

[Sure thing,] Henry replied.

~

Jim came back to the Tesseract just after dinner.

"Okay, we are done here," he told John.

"Wow, that was fast," John noted.

"Yes, it was. Mariah's idea to put a full-blown AI doctor software into them eliminates a whole bunch of training."

"Jessica, is everyone back on board?"

"Yes, sir. I have a full green check-in panel."

"Good, then button her up, and let's get back into orbit."

The Tesseract lifted off. Orbit was twenty minutes away. John recomputed the orbit to sync this time with York. When they arrived in their new orbital slot, John had Jim call down to the people at York.

"Herman," Jim addressed him. "We are in orbit."

"Well, it's a bit late now. I thought you would be here sooner."

"Yeah, I thought so, too. The captain didn't tell me we would arrive this late. We will have to come down tomorrow morning."

"I will see you then," Herman told him in closing.

~

The public landing pad at York was right next to the beach on the southern edge of town. There was a brisk onshore breeze blowing that gave Jessica a challenge with her spot-on landing, but she was up to that. Kip's fighter stayed in orbit this time to keep from complicating matters any more than they already were. John was not showing these York folks any more than he had to, as a precaution.

There was a small committee there to greet Jim as he exited the gangway, followed by Henry and the android carrying the crate. This time there was a transport waiting, too. Andy loaded the crate into the transport while Jim and Henry got into the passenger compartment. Andy crawled into the cargo compartment. He wasn't proud. John and Mariah watched them all leave.

Everyone walked the hundred meters or so to the beach, so the wait was going to be a pleasant one. The girls played in the sand at the nearby beach under Sam's watchful eyes. Mariah and Jessica were 'catching the rays' and enjoying the refreshing sea breeze. John used the ring to bring Kip down for the day. Kip brought his bathing suit and a big smile.

Jane sent her android to the beach with towels and a mess tent. Kip ran right into the surf. The girls ran to the edge but didn't go in past their knees. Sam was with them every step anyway. Everyone was duly shocked that John came along to the beach to enjoy the sand, and the waves, and the sea breeze in his hair. He swam for a bit in the surf, and let Sophie and Emma bury him in the sand when he laid down next to Mariah. As long as John was watching the girls, Sam went for a swim with Kip.

"Every delivery should be this rough," Mariah commented to Jessica.

At lunchtime, Jane set out another of her wonderful barbecue feasts on

Henry's makeshift grill. They had charcoal grilled hamburgers and hot dogs, hot and cold potato salads, and those bread-and-butter pickles that everyone loved. For the first time, Mariah failed to complain about it not being safe to eat food burned on an open fire.

After Jane's android carried all of the leftovers back to the ship, even Jane had time to sit and relax. She relaxed in the shade of the mess tent. It had open sides, so she could see all around and enjoy the view and the breeze, but she much preferred the shade than sitting in the sun, as she tended to burn rather than tan.

~~~

Henry and Jim went quite a way in the transport to a very modern-looking building across town from the seaside landing pad. Everything went as expected. Andy uncrated the Mini-Medlab. Doctor Jim went through a full demonstration for Herman's medical people. They all tried it and were very satisfied. They gave Herman's man the nod that all was well.

"Doctor, will you all please follow me," he told them. They all walked down a long, narrow corridor. Before they knew what was happening, Henry and Jim were trapped.

"What the hell?" Henry yelled at whoever was listening. He banged on the door with his fist.

"What's going on?" Jim asked Henry.

"Looks like we are prisoners," Henry told him. "They bottled us up here to cut my Mindlink off from the android, so we can't even call for help."

"Well, that sucks," Jim commented. "What do we do?"

"We sit here and wait," was all Henry could think to do, and so they did.

~~~

[Alarm,] Henry's android sent back to the Tesseract when the door in front of him slammed shut and he lost his wi-fi connection with Henry's Mindlink. Angel transferred the network call directly to John while she prepped the ship, just in case.

[What's wrong, Andy?] John quickly responded.

[The door in front of me slammed shut. I lost contact with Henry's Mindlink. There are men in the next room with pulse rifles. They are speaking in harsh tones.]

Now that got John's attention.

[Red Alert!] John sounded the alarm. "Everyone back to the ship. This is not a drill."

They all scrambled back on board and took their battle stations. Kip went to the ring room to quantum portal himself back up to his ship. Mariah quickly took her seat and scanned Andy's near coordinates. It did look like Henry and Jim were close-by, sitting on the floor. Just as Andy warned them, there were men close by with pulse rifles.

~~~

Jim was shocked to see a shimmering wall of light suddenly appear out of nowhere, but Henry recognized it immediately.

"Come on, Jim. We're leaving."

"We are?" he asked but followed Henry through the wall of light to find himself in the ring room, with John waiting for them.

"We have to get Andy out of there," Henry told John.

"I am already working on that," John replied.

[Andy, when the shimmering wall of light appears, walk straight into it.] Henry instructed his android buddy. Moments later, Andy emerged from the ring, and John closed the wormhole.

[Mariah, love, have you found their bank yet?]

[Yes, dear, passing you the coordinates,] she replied. They popped up on the ring display. John selected them.

"Jim, make them out a paid receipt for the full amount. How much is that?"

"That would be 250,000 Union Dollars, in hard currency."

John went back to his ring controls as Jim wrote the receipt on his tablet and printed a hard copy to the office printer. Henry sent his android to fetch it. John zeroed in on the bank vault and a stack of Union $1,000 gold coins. Jim and Henry counted out the 255 gold coins for the cost of the unit plus shipping. Jim slipped the receipt back into the pile where the
~~~

gold had once been.

[Lift off,] John told Jessica as he made his way to the bridge. [Let's get the hell out of here.]

Jim followed John while everyone else took their normal battle stations. John let Jim take one of the jump seats on the bridge, so he could watch them leave. Sophie and Emma had their bridge seats next to Mariah, where she knew they would be safe.

That would have been the end of this sorry episode, except that those arrogant York SOBs actually had the unmitigated gall to fire on the Tesseract as she departed. That sincerely pissed John off, so he took the helm and turned the ship back hard around. He spent the next ten minutes pounding their town hall into oblivion with his pulse cannons. Jessica could have sworn that he was enjoying himself the whole time.

"I hope those assholes get the picture of who you can screw with and who you can't," were John's parting words. "But they did have one nice beach, though."

That made Jim laugh. "I can't believe through all of that you kept your sense of humor."

"Sense of humor?" John teased him. "It was a nice beach." They all laughed.

"Jim, John doesn't know how to relax, but this time, even he was enjoying that beach."

"Yeah, but just like my mother always told me: 'Too much joy comes to grief.'"

"My mother told me that too when I got rowdy," Jim confessed.

"I never got too rowdy," Jessica told them.

"Well, I sure did," Mariah admitted.

"Oh, yeah. Go figure," Jessica teased her.

"She still is pretty rowdy," John told them.

She raised a clenched fist at him and threatened, "Pow! Zoom!"

"Mom!" Sophie scolded her with a wagging finger, "How many times do I have to tell you – no hitting?"

"She has to defend him even if he deserves to get hit," Emma explained to Jim. "He's her Ka."

The Tesseract joined back up with the other ships in orbit about the same time that Jane put out the picnic leftovers from the beach for dinner, along with some freshly made hamburgers and hot dogs. They weren't cooked over an open fire, so they lacked that smoky, open barbeque flavor. As everyone moved to the mess for dinner, Jim found it strangely comforting how this odd concoction of characters took this life of danger with such a joyful attitude.

Jim thought that he had an outworlds upbringing, but his life was tame compared to this. On the other hand, the incomplete end of the war had left the far outworlds in chaos, torn between two lifestyles, littered with the human debris of war. 'Making a difference starts with me' was beginning to sound pretty good to him.

Chapter Thirteen
The road to hell.

"Is a starship a pretty decent home?" Jim asked the girls at breakfast.

Emma explained to him, "This is not a home; it's an adventure."

"She tells that to everybody who asks," Sophie explained to Jim.

"But it's true," Emma insisted. "When I wasn't living in some awful hole in the ground, I was kept in a locked room or even worse – locked in a shipping container, all alone. Then my father found me, and that changed everything. Every day is an adventure on the Tesseract."

"I have to agree with you, Emma. From what I have seen so far, it looks that way to me."

Sam, who was normally very quiet, entered the conversation. "Life on the Tesseract is what you make of it. It can be an adventure if you make it an adventure."

"As in, 'making a difference starts with me'?"

"See, you do understand," Sam concluded. Sam could see in Jim's face what was going on in his head. "If you do decide to make a difference, you could really use some physical conditioning. Why don't you come down to the war games for a workout with me after breakfast? At least that way, you can see where you stand. Besides, the war game is great combat training, and you sure could use some of that where this ship goes."

"Oh, doctors are non-combatants," Jim gave Sam his canned response.

"So, how did that work for you on Renselar-7?"

"Heat of the moment," Jim claimed, "and the possibility that those reptilians had no clue what a non-combatant was."

"Actually, you were right. Those god-awful reptilians have no clue what the hell a non-combatant is, and I don't think they would have given a rat's ass even if they did."

"Maybe I had better go down to the war games with you," Jim

conceded.

~

Angel sat on the bridge alone in the wee hours of the night. She had just selected the next waypoint and was waiting for the other copilots to lock fields for the jump when the pilot's station suddenly lit up on its own. She watched in utter amazement as the pilot's station reset the course and propagated it out to the other ships. All of the ships locked fields. Suddenly, the laser engine modification lit up, and the entire Tesseract Fleet started flying the course in harmonic timequake mode. The speed indicator showed C35.756.

[Iyo?]

[*Yes. Call the captain.*]

[Captain! Emergency! Please come to the bridge right away!] Angel called him.

John was out of bed, grabbing underwear, shorts, and a tee-shirt, and dressing on the run before he was even fully awake.

"What's the problem?" he asked Angel as he arrived, but it quickly became apparent to him. He could see the stars moving quickly by. He could see the speed indicator for himself.

"The pilot's station just lit up and did all this," she told him. "So, I called you right away."

John looked at the course and scratched his head. "I wonder why we are headed for such a remote waypoint."

"What should I tell the other copilots? They are all ablaze to know what's going on."

What is the worst-case scenario here?

[Where are you sending me?] John asked into the open network.

[*To save more souls,*] came back his answer. This voice was female.

This was like that damned mysterious error message, only this time it was even more direct. John trusted the anoza, or whatever, or whoever the hell was telling him this. He looked at the course data on the pilot's station's display and scratched his head for a few seconds.

"We will reach the plotted course endpoint at 08:57 Zulu," John told

Angel. "When we do, I want all ships at battle stations on Red Alert."

Kip's bleary-eyed face appeared on his main bridge display. "John, my man, what the hell is going on? Rachel woke me up all upset, and I found my ship… flying at C35.756."

"Look at your course display. We are being sent to rescue somebody there. We will arrive at 08:57 Zulu. Expect some real trouble when we get there."

"Rescue somebody? Who? From what?"

"Damned if I know," John told him.

"Damned if you know? Then how did you know to go there?"

"You don't want to know," he told Kip. "I am still figuring that one out myself."

"Oh," was all Kip could say to that. "Well, when you finally do figure it out, then tell me. In the meantime, I am going to plunk my ass right here on my bridge and get some shut-eye." The connection closed.

"Should I wake Jessica?" Angel asked.

"No. Let them all sleep. There is nothing they can do right now anyway. Wait until 07:00; then wake them all up. I need everybody fresh and alert for our arrival onsite at 08:57 Zulu."

"What about you?" she asked.

"I am going to sleep right here in my chair. Wake me if you need me." He shut his eyes and did the best he could to rest with what was going on around him.

"Captain," Angel's soft voice gently woke him. "I am getting everyone else up now."

John gave them until 07:15 to announce, "All hands, all hands, there is an emergency meeting in the mess at 07:30."

[What's going on?] Mariah immediately had to know.

[Yeah, what's the emergency?] Jessica had to know, too.

[We are on an emergency rescue mission. I will tell everyone the whole story in the mess.]

Oh, yeah. Like that was a sufficient answer for those two. Jessica called Angel, with Mariah listening to her every word. Needless to say, John expected as much but was just as happy. Retelling this story was way too many words for him, and the ladies did not seem to have a short version of anything. So, let Angel give them the blow-by-blow details. It would save him endless long explanations with way too many words. At least that was the plan.

Everyone arrived in the mess to find John pounding down a couple of breakfast burritos and his third cup of java. Humans are creatures of habit. Each had their own place. The table was set. Each place had that person's usual breakfast.

"Captain says everyone needs to eat a hearty breakfast. You are going to need it," Jane told each one as they arrived. Henry, Sam, and Jim were good with that and dug right in without so much as a word, but oh no, not Mariah and Jessica.

"Come on," Mariah complained. "You said there was a meeting."

"After breakfast," John said between bites. "I am sure that you already know most of it anyway, so don't waste time, eat."

"Ooh, Men! All they ever think about is food!" Mariah just had to grex as she sat down to her oatmeal and tea. Jessica didn't complain; she sat down and ate.

John finished his breakfast, took a big swallow of java, and began while everyone else was eating, "Angel, please broadcast this to all ships. At 08:57 Zulu, we will arrive onsite. All that I know right now is that we are being sent to save some souls. I have to assume the worst. We will arrive on Red Alert, at battle stations. The fighters will deploy into a full forward attack formation. I will call the friendlies and bogies as best I can."

"Sent? By who?" Jessica asked.

"The same 'who' that sent us the error message that saved our ship in the Seven Pillars."

"Oh, I see," Mariah said for both her and Jessica.

As the minutes ticked away, the tension grew. At T minus one minute, a countdown timer displayed in every ship's main display.

At zero, the Fleet entered normal space as the UV lasers shut down.

There before them sat two skeleton ships: half freight containers, half passenger cubes, and obviously dead in space. Their transponders ID'ed them as the Serenity and the Amazonas. They were being severely pounded by two frigate class vessels with no transponder returns, obviously not military, and four older-looking fighters. John quickly marked the bogies and the friendlies.

"Pirates!" John called over the com.

"Kip, lead the fighters. Barbie, take his wing. Lisa, lead Ann and Ciara. I will take one the frigates. They haven't spotted us yet." Kip led the M-4s into their second deep space battle. The M-4 copilots were getting very good at this.

While the Serenity was dead in the water, it appeared that the Amazonas was in some more serious trouble. The pirates had docked a fighter to it.

The Tesseract bore down hard on the pirate frigate attacking the Amazonas, seriously damaging one of the frigate's engines with the new rail-gun cannons, but that was too easy. While the Tesseract maneuvered, it took a pounding from the second frigate's pulse-cannons. Much to John's surprise, the first frigate was still able to maneuver away. The pirates had apparently figured out the need for a second set of engines.

John swung the Tesseract hard about to run on the second pirate frigate, but its captain used the damaged passenger ships as a shield. Kip and Barbie, having made short order out of the old fighters, picked up the chase on the second frigate. It severely pounded them with its pulse-cannons. Its captain had to question why they did not even bother with shields, until he realized how useless his pulse-cannons were against them.

About then, John came around the passenger ships to the frigate's flank. John let go a furious barrage of rail-gun fire at the frigate's flank, damaging the ship, only to have him jump out. The first frigate joined in the retreat seconds later.

[Barbie, fly over to the Amazonas and connect to their wi-fi. Get us connected.]

[Yes, sir.] She flew over. [Sorry, Captain. No network.]

[Kip, I don't know if those pirates are coming back.]

[Fighters, form a perimeter on high alert,] Kip commanded.

"I have 57 life signs in the Amazonas," Mariah reported, "…and pulse weapons fire." She looked hard at John.

Sam came scrambling to the ring room with John's recon armor in hand, pulse rifles, and a couple of shotguns slung over his shoulder. John suited up while Mariah dialed the quantum portal into the passenger ship. John and Sam ran through the ring.

~~~

Mariah had quantum portaled them into the main corridor running down the backbone of the ship. It was dimly lit by emergency lights only, giving it an eerie look. The air was thin; life support was down. A thin haze of smoke with the acrid smell of something electrical burning hung in the thin air. At the far end, they could just barely make out four men with weapons.

[Mariah, where was that pulse fire?]

[At the far end of the corridor from you.]

In the distance, John could see the men pounding on a door and shooting at it. They were dressed for battle and looked tough as nails. They sure did not look at all like colonists.

[Sam, those men look like pirates.] John and Sam started advancing on the men, firing at them as they advanced. Two of the men turned and returned fire while the other two kept working on the door, but John and Sam wore personal shields. They closed relentlessly on the pirates. In the face of John and Sam's relentless advance, the other two pirates gave up working on the door to fire on John and Sam. At close range, John pulled his shotgun over his shoulder. So did Sam. They just kept firing until all of the pirates were down.

John looked at the door. The pirates had it all but down. John gave it a kick. It collapsed inside the room beyond. The people beyond the door all screamed.

"It's okay, folks!" John yelled in. "We are the good guys."

"Did you kill the pirates?" one little boy asked him as he and Sam
~~~

walked in.

"Some of them," John told him. "Folks, I need your help to get this ship moving again."

"We are farmers and settlers," one man told John. "We are not starship engineers."

"We have wounded people here," a woman in the back called out to him.

"I will have to get my doctor and engineer over here," John decided out loud.

[Mariah, we have wounded. We need Jim and Henry over here on the double.]

Five minutes later, the quantum portal's shimmering circular wall appeared. Henry's android walked through with a Mini-Medlab, followed by Jim and Henry. John went back the other way to the Tesseract.

~~~

John shed his recon armor and weapons in the ring room but left them there, just in case. He went to the bridge, took his seat, and commanded, [Tactical.]

"They are still out there somewhere," Mariah told him quietly.

"Jim, how are you doing?" John asked him through the com.

"Not good. I have five dead, not counting the pirates you shot, and seven wounded -- three seriously. I am sending one of those back through the ring with Sam to your Medlab."

"The entire flight crew on the Amazonas is either dead or seriously wounded," Henry reported to John. "I have one engine here beyond fixing. They do have a spare in stores, but with no help, I am not sure how much good that will do me."

"Tesseract, Tesseract. This is Captain Hannibal Jones of the Serenity," they were being hailed. "I don't know how to thank you, sir. Those pirates were about to kill us all."

"How is your ship? Is it spaceworthy?"

"We had two hull breaches, but I think that we have that under control now. Our reactors went down when our shields gave out. My engineer was
~~~

wounded, but he is currently directing the effort to get us back up."

"Your companion ship is down for the count. Do you have room on board for 50 more passengers?"

"Room I have, life support I don't," Captain Jones replied.

"Let me work on that," John told Captain Jones.

"Henry," John called him. "Do I remember correctly that life support on these skeleton ships is nothing more than a module?"

"Yes, sir. That is correct. What are you thinking?"

"If the Amazonas' life support module is still working, we move it and the people over to the Serenity. That ship has a full crew, and their engines are intact."

Henry considered that for a few seconds. "Before we decide to do that, let me see if this life support is any good."

"Okay, that works for me. You have the ball on this project. Keep me posted."

"Kip, did you read the jump wakes on those frigates?"

"Sure as shooting," he replied. "They jumped off to a waypoint with a habitable planet."

"Oh, good. That is just what we need. They must have a whole pirate's den out here. Can you please take Lisa and recon that?"

"You got it," Kip replied. Seconds later, he and Lisa left.

~~~

On the Amazonas, Henry was scrambling. It took him almost an hour, but he managed to get the main reactor back up. With that, the ship's main lights came back on, and the computers all rebooted. Henry got his first overall look at the whole ship on the engineer's display. Life support came right online and ran. At least that was good news. A lot of what he was looking at was not, but the captain's plans were to abandon this ship, so there was no sense in wasting time.

[Captain,] Henry called over to the Tesseract, [the life support system here is fine. I am going to get air quality up as best I can to give us time to move these people. I am estimating two hours at full output to get that done.]
~~~

[How long to pull the module and install it on the Serenity?]

[From what I see, it should be an hour to pull it and another hour to install it.]

Four hours is an eternity in any battle. John had to juggle all of this in his head.

[Henry, you can run the life support for one hour. Then, pull it.]

[Uh, that's cutting it very thin,] Henry advised him.

[I know. That means that I will have to start moving people right away. I also need you to set some things up for me.]

[Evil things?] Henry asked with a hint of mischief in his voice.

[Definitely evil things.]

[You know how I love being someone's worse nightmare,] Henry reminded John as he got to it.

John turned to Jessica and Mariah. "I need you two to go to the ring room and start moving those people right away. I need you to move all of the people over to the Serengeti in the next hour or so. Angel, you have the helm."

"Move families first?" Mariah asked.

"Women and children first," John agreed, "keeping families together as best we can." Then John had another thought. "In an emergency, get them all over here on the Tesseract. We can deal with the consequences when the emergency is over."

"What can our life support handle," Jessica asked, "just in case."

"We could take on 30 people or so for the long haul, but 57 will definitely overload life support in a day or so. Move as many as you can, like I said, to the Serenity." That was the plan – move the people. Mariah and Jessica went to the ring room. Mariah dialed up the Amazonas, and Jessica went over.

<p style="text-align:center">~~~</p>

Jessica stepped out of the ring right into the room where all the people were gathered. Jim was working on the wounded in one corner. She didn't see Henry. She walked up to an apparent family group, but a nice-looking older man walked over to greet her.

"Hello, my name is Micah. Everyone here is afraid and confused, but they trust me. What can I do to help?"

"Micah, I am Jessica. This ship is dead in space. We need to move the people over to the Serenity, but they will have to move in small groups. Families with children should go first."

Micah explained all of that to the assembled group. Micah knew them all. He knew them well. He chose the first family and sent them to Jessica. Jessica sent them through the ring to Mariah on the Tesseract. Mariah then sent them on to the Serenity. So, it began. The next group went through.

Micah mumbled, "The road to Hell is paved with good intentions."

"What do you mean by that?" Jessica asked him.

"It was a premonition," Micah whispered. "Please forgive me. It wasn't meant for your ears. I am curious. What brought you to us? How did you find us?"

"I am not exactly sure," Jessica told him even though she knew damned well.

Micah smiled. "You were the answer to my prayer," he told her.

"Or to your emergency beacon," Jessica replied as they sent another family through.

"So, are you a minister? A priest?" Jessica inquired.

"No, but a holy man, of sorts," Micah replied.

"And these people are your flock?" Jessica pushed the issue.

"Oh, heavens no. I am just traveling with them… to keep them safe from evil."

[I am about to disconnect the life support,] Henry told Jessica, [so the lights will flicker when I do it. You had better warn everybody, so they know it's all right.]

"Micah, my ship's engineer is telling me to warn everyone that he is doing some work and the lights will flicker, but that is not a bad thing."

Micah announced that just ahead of the lights flickering, but they all gasped anyway.

~~~

The bridge of the Tesseract came alive with the call from Kip.
~~~

[Red Alert! Red Alert!] Kip called through the network to John. [I am trailing four pirate frigates headed your way.]

[Pirates headed our way,] John told everyone on the network.

~~~

"Micah," Jessica whispered to him, "trouble is on the way. We are out of time. We need to get these people through as quickly as possible now."

As calm as could be, Micah told the folks, "We are going to try this differently. Let's all just line up and go through that shining wall of glory. No panic. Just different." That worked. Everyone followed Micah's instructions. Jessica, Micah, and Jim each helped a wounded passenger through the portal. Henry had left his android with Doctor Jim when he went aboard Barbie's M-4 to transfer the life support pod, so Andy was the last one back through the portal, carrying the Mini-Medlab.

~~~

It would have been total pandemonium with 32 new people aboard the Tesseract but for Micah. The folks trusted him. Mariah and Jane both worked with Micah to move each family into a room and get them settled, at least temporarily.

The bridge of the Tesseract prepared once more for battle. Jessica took her seat and prepared to maneuver as John studied his tactical display.

[Henry, how are you doing with that life support module?]

[I am just fitting it into place on the Serenity as we speak,] he replied. [Ten minutes. Give me ten more minutes.]

[We will do our best,] John told him.

"Captain Hannibal, is your ship ready to maneuver?" John asked him.

"I am told we are about ready to give it a try," he responded.

"You are out of time. There are four pirate frigates on hard approach. My engineer will push the life support module into place in the next few minutes. When that is done, you absolutely have to jump out. I sent you over a very specific course. Whatever you do, do not vary from that exact course until we all join back up. Now, please hold for my countdown. All of the ships will jump out at the same time to cover your jump wake."

"A trick from the war?" Captain Hannibal asked.

"Yes, it is," John confirmed.

[John,] Kip's voice once more came through the network, [two ships broke off from the group. It looks to me like they are trying to outflank you. Twenty minutes to contact.]

The seconds ticked away as John waited for Henry to finish his task.

"The life support pod is secure. I have a green light to maneuver," Captain Hannibal reported. "I have a positive engine test. We are all set."

[Henry, where are you?] Jessica called over the network.

[I am with Barbie, love. I am fine.]

[Barbie, you watch him. He has wandering hands,] Jessica warned her.

[He has very nice hands,] Barbie replied, not at all getting what Jessica implied.

The girl is a ditz, Jessica could not help but think. *A nice ditz, but still, a ditz.*

[All ships, converge on the Serenity,] John commanded. The M-4s converged.

[On my mark, scatter. Serenity, on my mark, jump out to your first waypoint… Mark.]

All of the ships scattered, and the Serenity jumped out.

The Tesseract came right back. She sat a distance from the now derelict skeleton ship and just waited. Suddenly, the first two pirate frigates broke into normal space and began maneuvering. Kip and Lisa were right on their heels.

[Kip, you and Lisa attack one of those ships. Give them something to worry about,] John commanded, and so this second engagement began. John picked up the attack on the second frigate. The pirates were obviously not used to picking on anyone actually able to defend themselves and so took a sound drubbing.

Just as Kip surmised, the second two frigates suddenly appeared on their flank.

[Now,] John commanded over the network.

The other M-4s suddenly reappeared and were all over those two frigates like white on rice. It wasn't pretty, but these were pirates. They deserved to get their asses handed to them. When one of the pirate frigates slipped behind the derelict skeleton ship, John sent a command through the network to send its remaining reactors into overload. The resulting explosion took out the pirate frigate as well.

[All ships, assemble,] John commanded. To that, all of the Tesseract ships fell back to assemble in formation around the Tesseract. They all locked fields. John engaged the UV lasers. The Tesseract fleet vanished before the remaining pirates' very eyes and flew away.

"Wow," Jessica commented. "That was way cool but come on. We really need a cool name for this way cool engine modification thing of yours."

The Codex files referred to this new drive as an harmonic timequake drive because of the way it moved through time-space.

"Slipstream drive!" Mariah suggested.

"Ooh, I like that," Jessica agreed.

"I like that, too. That name would not expose any technical secrets," John had to agree.

"Okay! Slipstream drive it is then," Jessica announced the verdict.

John checked his engineering display. Life support showed both the primary and secondary systems running at 98%. That was pushing it a bit, but better than he expected. The third system showed its status as 'Hot Standby.' It was hard to keep in mind that the Tesseract was originally a frigate-class ship before they wrecked it. It was designed for this many people.

CHAPTER FOURTEEN
Legend of the fall.

For the first time ever, the Tesseract's mess was full to overflowing with people. The overflow crowd filled the lounge. Jane was in joyous overload trying to feed all of these people but also challenged to stretch what she had for this many hungry mouths. Believe me, she was more than up to that challenge. There was a glow on her face that gave away how happily she faced this test of her culinary skills.

People overflowed into the lounge. Down one deck, they overflowed into the hold. There was a somber tone to their voices and a sadness on their faces. Through this, Micah noted, walked Sophie and Emma. They brought with them a basket of cholate chip cookies and an armload of dolls. They joyfully dispersed their own dollies to the younger girls who looked like they could use a friend right now, but everyone got a hug and a cookie.

"We were rescued by a fleet of warrior angels," Micah said mostly to himself.

"I am very proud of my daughters," Mariah replied to that very quietly.

"Angels in the truest sense," Micah agreed.

"Jessica said that you are a holy man. Shouldn't you be praying or preaching or something?" Mariah asked him.

"Not really. I am not that kind of a holy man," Micah admitted.

"Well then, what kind of a holy man are you?" John asked as he came from the bridge for a break as much as another cup of java.

"The same kind as you," he told a surprised John.

"Me? How would that be?" John wanted to know.

"What would it profit a man if he gained the entire world but lost his soul?" Micah tested him with a question.

John smiled and took on that familiar challenge. "I have something more precious than all the gold of many worlds – a loving wife and daughters, loving friends in abundance, and a righteous purpose to my life."

"See! I knew it! This is your soul, and you know it! You feel it in your heart, in every part of your being. And your feet were set on this path. You were chosen. Whether you know it or not, in your own way, you are a holy man too, just like me," Micah concluded.

"I chose this path myself," John challenged Micah's facts. "And I am hardly a holy man."

"Did you choose this path by your own free will, or was it by fate?" Micah asked him.

"A little of both, I would think," John gave him his best estimate.

"But fate and free-will are two sides of the same coin. You were chosen. You were set on this path." Then Micah hesitated. He seemed a bit confused for a second before he ventured to say, "Like Job in the Old Testament, you had to lose everything to become what you are today."

"What? How could you possibly know that?" John asked him. Mariah winced.

"Words sometimes find my mouth their willing servant," Micah admitted. "I didn't know how that applied to you, but you just confirmed to me that it does."

To Mariah's great surprise, John took in a deep breath and let it out. With it came all of those gripping emotions and terrible pain. They dispersed into the air along with that breath.

"What kind of holy man are you?" John asked him after that.

"Me? I am just a humble servant and not a very good one at that. I run out of words when I pray, and I couldn't preach a sermon to save my own soul," Micah told him, "but people trust me. They know that I am honest, sometimes to my own detriment. They know that I will always do my best to protect them from evil. They know that I read the holy scriptures," he concluded with a smile.

"The Bible?" Mariah asked.

"And the Zenobian Zenotra and the Yarjin Tahara," Micah told her.

"What set your feet on the path?" John turned his own question on him.

"Many years ago," Micah recounted, "I was but a young Fleet officer. I was assigned to the deep space exploration vessel Bark Star of India. Our mission – to find Earth. I was all hopped up for that; let me tell you. We brought the finest Earth scholars and stellar cartographers from all over the Union for that mission."

"Before I left, my grandmother put a copy of the Bible on my tablet and made me promise to read it. When one of the Earth scholars found me reading it one day, he told me what an incredible historical record it actually was. He added several more books to my tablet, all about the Bible as history. So here I was, all hopped up to begin with, and now encouraged by one of the most respected Earth Scholars in the entire Union, Professor Glen Markot. I devoured that material. I read every word. He grilled me every day on what I read. I could not have received a better education in any University in the entire Union."

"But I heard that voyage was a failure," John interjected.

"That is not the way we saw it. According to the stellar cartographers, we nailed it spot on," Micah continued, "but later, they were all second-guessing themselves. What might have once been Earth was nothing but a burned-out cinder. The planet that should have been Jupiter was missing, and the other outer planets were in complete orbital disarray. Even the star's spectrum was not exactly right for a G-Class star."

"Then it wasn't a failure," John concluded. "Something catastrophic happened."

"That was exactly what Professor Markot said. In fact, he quoted the scriptures. 'And I saw a new heaven and a new earth: for the first heaven and the first earth were passed away; and there was no more sea.' But, you know, for as intelligent as all of those other people were, they couldn't see the 800-pound roratan in the room."

"I was shocked and disillusioned, as was Professor Markot when the science team declared the mission to find Earth a failure. Hell, the stellar cartographers had even confirmed that the constellations, as viewed from the third planet and adjusted back in time, were all perfectly in accordance with all of the old records."

"Then, the mission to find Earth was actually a total success," John concluded, "but they didn't like what they found."

"You got that right. The political people assigned to the mission were all afraid of the consequences of people finding out what actually did happen, so they decided to keep 'Earth' a legend instead."

"Micah, is it possible that you saved those galactic coordinates?" John asked.

A smile crossed Micah's face. "Yes, of course, I did." He pulled his trusty old, timeworn tablet from his pocket and called up the data. John had the network server pull the data and send it to his star charts marked 'Earth.' There was a huge smile on John's face.

"Someday, you will go there," Micah told him. "You will confirm that Earth is found."

"Yes, I will," John affirmed. "And you can take that to the bank."

"Just remember," Micah told his new friend, "'Earth' is all around you now."

"What do you mean by that?" John just had to know.

"You have to remember that I studied the Bible as history," Micah prefaced his response. "So, whether you take this as historical fact or religion, I will leave that up to you. First, Isaiah was told: 'For behold, I create new heavens and a new earth; And the former things will not be remembered or come to mind.' That was later reaffirmed to John: 'Then I saw a new heaven and a new Earth; for the first heaven and the first earth passed away, and there is no longer any sea.' But you have to keep in mind that those ancient people had no idea how many 'Earths' there really were. They only understood 'Earth' in the singular. But now we know better than that. In fact, there are many new Earths, but now for the hard part – humans were cast into the outer darkness because of the evil in our hearts," Micah warned him.

"So, I have been told, but there are so many good people out here," John protested.

"You see the enigma within the mystery!" Micah pushed his thinking. "Humans are once more being sifted through the sands of time to separate the good from the evil, but this time on many Earths and in all the heavens. Wow! I can't wait to see how this turns out!"

"Do you believe all of that?" Mariah asked him quietly as they returned to the bridge.

"In my own way, I guess I do," John told her. "I was never a very religious person. My mother was. She made me learn all of that, and I do believe that I am a better man for it."

John took his seat, but he was so caught up in the whole 'Earth' discussion that he could not resist looking at it on his own star charts. To his amazement, 'Sol' and 'Earth' had already been correctly placed and named on the charts. It was marked as new data from Ishmael Tobruk's tablet.

"Mariah, love, look at this!" he called her over to see for herself.

Mariah could not believe what she was seeing, but there it was.

"The Syndicate knew that it was there all along," John concluded. He got back up to go find Micah. He was still in the mess.

"Get out your tablet," John told him. Micah was a bit puzzled but complied.

"I just discovered that Earth's existence was independently confirmed by the famous deep space explorer, Ishmael Tobruk, and handed down seven generations from father to son. It was given to me as a personal favor. I didn't even realize that I had it until just a few minutes ago. I am giving you a copy." The network server downloaded Ishmael's data to Micah's tablet. Micah just looked in total disbelief at the independent confirmation that he now held in his hand of Earth's existence.

"After all these many years, despite what people said, I am not a crazy man," Micah declared.

"Oh, yes you are, but you are crazy in a good way," John teased him, "and I am too."

CHAPTER FIFTEEN
New Earth.

Finding the skeleton ship, Serenity, was less of a problem than John had anticipated. Henry had sent one of his micro-bots to make up the final connections on the life support system, not trusting that job to the Serenity's overworked, wounded chief engineer. That micro-bot had a quantum-com module on it as well as wi-fi.

When the time came to transfer all of the passengers to the Serenity, Mariah fired up the ring, but the whole crew was there to say goodbye to their guests. Sophie and Emma made sure to hug all of the children and wish them well. Doctor Jim had to ask each of his patients how they were doing one last time. Sam mostly smiled at the girls. Some of the older single girls just had to kiss him goodbye, and that was fine by Sam.

Last to leave was Micah. He gave Jessica a big hug and Mariah too, before turning to John.

"My path, for now, is with these people," he told John.

"Like you, I go wherever I am needed," John told him. "Where exactly are you headed?"

"New Earth, of course, New Earth," he told John with a big smile.

They shook hands, and Micah took one last look around before he stepped through the ring.

For hours, all that could be heard was the sound of Jane's task-bots cleaning. Everyone was exhausted. Sophie and Emma went right to bed. Mariah wasn't far behind. Sam intended to go for a workout but ended up taking a nap first. Doctor Jim was beyond exhaustion. He was asleep on a couch in the lounge when John passed by. He was so sound asleep that the task-bots cleaning around him did not disturb him one bit. Jessica and Henry were nowhere to be found, and John was not about to ask the system to locate them as he headed for the bridge.

Angel smiled at him when he took his seat. John sat for a while just looking at the data for Earth that Micah gave him. It coincided exactly with the data from Ishmael's tablet.

Why did the Syndicate want to keep Earth's location a secret? That just did not make any logical sense to him. Micah told him that humans were cast into the outer darkness because of the evil in their hearts. Goodness and truth love the light, but evil loves the darkness. Evil hates the truth and thrives in darkness.

I would be one sorry-ass excuse for a 'holy man.' I swear like a trooper. Hell, I was one. I took my pound of flesh. I harbor hate to the very core of me; I hate Sarsen Tabbot. I love to have a few beers and a good bar fight every now and then. I am sure not very religious at all. And chosen? Who in their right mind would choose me?

But the long hours had taken their toll on John too. He closed his eyes for just a minute but fell asleep for what would be hours. Angel saw her Captain sleeping in his seat. She took out a warm fleece to cover him. When she put the fleece over him, she saw a message on his display and smiled …

Leaf in the wind, I chose you.

"So, you said," Angel whispered.

~

"Captain, we need to reprovision," Jane informed him over his cup of java and breakfast burritos the next day, "or we will be eating rice and beans the rest of the way home."

"Oh crap. We can't have that," John agreed.

"Jane says we are out of food," John told Mariah when she came to the mess.

"Oh, well, now there is an emergency if I ever saw one," She commented jokingly.

"We have another emergency?" Jessica asked from the portal as she came in for breakfast.

"We're out of food," John told her. Jessica was no slouch at packing away the chow either, so she quickly saw the 'emergency' to the situation, too.

"I need to find us a suitable world not too far off our path home," John told them.

Mariah let out a deep sigh. "I really should do that job myself. You would find the closest planet with hotdogs that you could burn on an open fire. I will find us a place with real food."

"Whatever you find," Jane assured them, "I will make do."

"I would much rather make do with some steak, and seafood, and some decent vegetables," Mariah insisted. "The girls need to eat right." Of course, she included herself in this particular invocation of 'the girls.'

Later, on the bridge, Mariah and Jessica worked that task together. Angel had already listed the worlds right along their path home, but Mariah called up the database with her own set of parameters to find Radion-4.

"It's only six hours away," Jessica confirmed, failing to tell John that it was the farthest out-of-the-way choice that Mariah could have made.

~~~

Radion-4 was fairly modern for as far off of the beaten path as it was, but that would be as compared to some of the incredibly crude places they had more recently visited. It did have an approach control protocol, but that was all handled by artificials. ILS pattern one landed them at the public landing pad at Mystic, the main small city, located right on the ocean. So, there was the real reason for Mariah and Jessica to connive this place to reprovision.

That would have worked well in their favor, but for the time of year it was on the planet's surface. The Tesseract and Kip's fighter landed in what could only be described as an impending storm. The clouds were dark, and there was a stiff breeze blowing. The pilots parked their ships facing away from the strong onshore breeze.

Mariah downloaded a GPS database from the City Hall.

"Hello folks," a pleasant woman's face appeared on the display. "I am the local Sheriff. Can you please state your business here?"

"We just need to resupply our ship's pantry," Jessica told her.

"Did you bring hard currency for that?" the woman asked.
~~~

"Yes, we did," Jessica replied.

"Good. Then we would kindly ask that you leave any firearms on your ship. The markets here won't open any doors for armed visitors."

"We will shop unarmed then," Jessica agreed.

"Very good. You will find all of the markets located under the dome. I suggest you shop online first, but you will have to pick up your supplies and pay in person. Sorry for the bad weather, but you did come at a bad time of the year here. Have a nice day and enjoy your stay on Radion-4. You might consider coming back some time in the summer when our weather is spectacular."

One more disappointment. Shop online is not what Mariah was expecting, but she and Jane got right to that task. There was no barter here. Prices were listed for each market but varied quite a bit.

"When prices vary that much, there has to be a difference in quality. We are just going to have to go look for ourselves," Jane told Mariah. "Besides, I like seeing and smelling and squeezing things myself."

"Yeah, me too," Mariah agreed, but she was more intent on squeezing some women's clothes, shoes, and accessories in the place right next to the market.

"Yeah, me too," Jessica agreed when she saw what Mariah had in mind.

Mariah had John get the LZ ready. John and Jim did not plan on going shopping with the ladies. Sam would go on full alert while they were gone. Kip was having way too much fun just standing outside next to the docks, with his face into the wind, enjoying the wind in his hair from the approaching storm.

John knew that he was in for more than he bargained for when all of the ladies came to the LZ dressed for a shopping spree, Sophie and Emma trailing behind, but he just smiled and got everyone on board.

Mariah pulled up the dome on the LZ's navigation system and set it as the destination.

[Confirmed,] she told it, and they were off. The LZ went right into the local traffic and quickly advanced on its destination. The domed structure was huge. The people living in Mystic had adapted to these storms. The domed structure even had inside parking to make spending your money in any weather as easy as they could.

John liked this place right away. While his ladies shopped, he could sit in an open pub under the dome and watch the people moving all around him. It even had Reuben sandwiches! How great was that? Jim went his own way but returned in an hour. He had bought some new shirts and a hand-tooled leather wallet, but that was it for him.

"I am all shopped out," he told John as he sat down. Jim ordered a tuna salad platter. It was three different tuna salads and a lot bigger than he expected. As he started to pick away at it, the ladies appeared. Jane's android led a trail of automated wagons carrying the food that Jane bought. While Jane's android led the wagon train of boxes and bags back to the LZ, the ladies helped Jim pick apart his way-too-big lunch platter. Refreshed and refueled, they quickly disappeared for round two.

John sat there, smiling the whole time.

"You seem to take their marathon shopping quite well," Jim commented.

"I am still laughing at them," he confided in Jim.

"For what?" Jim was puzzled.

"They think I don't know that they tried to snooker me. They took us way the hell off course trying to get another vacation on a sunny beach."

"Oh, yeah? Well, that didn't work out," Jim had to agree.

"Then they were not real happy to have to shop online," John still smiled.

"Oh, but this place had to redeem the side trip. This is like shopping on one of the pilgrim planets," Jim had to remind him.

"Yes, it is. So, once more, they thought they won, but here I sit, eating a Reuben and trying a local beer. So, it looks like it worked out for everybody, not perfect, but okay."

"Yes, I guess it did," Jim had to agree.

"So, how did things work out for you?" John asked him.

"Oh, I just bought a few small things," Jim quickly replied.

"I was thinking more about the trip in general," John changed gears.

"Oh, wow. It was way more than I ever expected," he told John. "I thought it would be endless hours and tediously boring."

John laughed. "Well, we certainly shot that expectation the hell out of the water."

Jim laughed. "Yes, you sure did. I never felt more alive in my whole life."

"And you're just going to return to your boring, humdrum life when we get back?"

"I have been meaning to talk to you about that," Jim replied.

"So, I hear," John told him. "Emma asked me if you could stay. I told her that you are more than welcome to stay, but that decision is up to you."

~~~

"Mom, can we keep Doctor Jim?" Emma asked Mariah in the midst of trying on some very nice, hand-tooled sandals. "I mean, we all like him, and he is very handy to have for medical things, like fixing you up when you get shot."

"Well, I am certainly not planning on getting shot anymore. He is welcome to stay, but that would only be if he wants to stay," Mariah answered her, "and if it is okay with your father."

Emma was about to tell her that she already checked with John, but Sophie saw that to be like poking a nest of angry bees and interjected, "Okay. We will ask him then, right Emma?" Emma could hardly miss the body English that Sophie was using to signal her 'ixnay!'

"Oh, yeah. We will ask him, then," Emma replied.

Mariah went on with her shopping, content in the knowledge that the girls would ask Jim to stay. She really liked Jim. Besides, he was a pretty good shot for a noncombatant, or so she heard.

~

For the most part, Radion-4 turned out to be an okay layover despite the weather. After a long, and I do mean shop-till-you-drop long, day shopping, the Tesseract once more cast itself into the outer darkness.

Jane cooked up one hell of a storm for dinner that evening. Kip came
~~~

over for the feast by way of the ring. It was a late dinner by outworld standards, but somehow John, Sam, Henry, and Kip each managed to eat their way through a huge lobster, a pile of the biggest shrimp they had seen in a long while, and some perfectly cooked fillet mignons. Everyone else ate well too, but without all of the people of recent days and no food fight, dinner seemed awfully quiet. The men let Jessica and Mariah talk them into trying a White Zinfandel that Mariah had bought on Radion-4. It was beyond outstanding.

Chapter Sixteen
No, the real outer darkness.

"Where there is challenge, there is opportunity," Al Simmonds reminded his people as they looked over the Treaty of Akheron. The Union had saved his sorry ass despite the loss of his light cruisers. His friends in the Union Senate had put enough pressure on Union Fleet to make it impossible for them to throw him to the dogs.

"I guess we now know what happened to Sarsen Tabbot, too," Frank offered. "The Union could not catch her or defeat her, so they tied her hand-and-foot to protect the other planets."

"I am not exactly sure what column that goes into, though," Al commented. "She was an asset at times, but a very expensive asset at that. In the end, she wasn't a very reliable asset either. For right now, I am going to have to put her loss into the plus column."

"I am puzzled, though," Frank continued. "Why didn't she go back and take Baratii-4 and Kharon-3 away from us?"

"I can answer that," a female voice offered. "You do not think at all like Mercs, or you would know that she would not act from some misplaced loyalty or patriotism. Instead, like a true Merc, she would have run a cost-benefit analysis to find that it was not worth her time or effort. They are too small for her to bother with. To her, your taking of them was a poor investment."

"And just how would you know that?" Al wanted to know.

"I am Myra Grantham. I used to be Chief Council when this was a Merc world before I was invited to join this Union government."

"Thank you, Myra. We appreciate your insight on this issue," Al told her. He knew that Frank had recruited any number of good people from the old government here with the right attitude – blatant self-interest.

"Okay, then," Al surmised. "We are back on plan. I want our people on

Baratii-4 and Kharon-3 to stop their damned bellyaching about an imminent invasion and get back to business. They know the plan. Come on. Execute, execute, execute."

"I will get right on that," Frank replied.

The plan that Al Simmonds referred to was formed with the information that Nikola kept had secret, only to himself. The secret was so well kept that Sarsen Tabbot saw no value in retaking Baratii-4 and Kharon-3 from him. The secret made Al Simmonds' future bright and sunny. Knowing it put a smile on his face.

~~~

Across the vastness of space, twelve newly commissioned skeleton freighters made way for the first time under the Harrier Interplanetary flag. They set course for the Seven Pillars.

~~~

Sarsen Tabbot sat quietly in her office. She had not come to this stage in her life to be ordered about by people so far inferior to her as to be ridiculous. It wasn't bad enough that the Merc forces had hired on as the Syndicate's military arm only to be defeated, but now the situation here beyond the Seven Pillars had turned to shit.

Life wasn't bad enough working for that filth Nikola until it got seriously worse working for that ever-conniving asshole, Al Simmonds. Now, even some pissant planetary politician on Akheron thought he could tell her what she could and could not do. She had worked much too hard her whole life to be reduced to the status of a mere public servant at this stage. Oh, no. That was not going to happen. In her own mind, Sarsen Tabbot was the Queen of War!

And as for her retaking of Baratii-4 and Kharon-3, well, they could go hold their hands on their asses and wait for that to happen for all that she cared. Why should she do what they wanted now? Even Union Fleet had given their tacit approval for her to retake Baratii-4 and Kharon-3 in the way they wrote the Treaty of Akheron. As far as she was concerned, that alone would have been reason enough for her not to.

~~~
~~~

The public landing pad at Akheron's largest city, Memphis, was not prepared for the sudden influx of heavy traffic. Shuttles and landing craft were quickly landing, dropping off their passengers, and returning to orbit for another round. People in uniforms, lugging all of their belongings in duffle bags, quickly flooded the well-lit terminal buildings.

Maryann Griffin, Malik's local representative, would not be deterred. Her medium frame and pleasant face did not do her tenacity justice. Boldly, she stood in the flow of people asking, "What is this all about? What is happening?" but no one cared to take the time to stop. She was a person of substantial importance. She was certainly not used to people ignoring her. In total frustration, she grabbed the arm of one fine-looking officer and walked with him.

"What is happening? Why are all these people here?"

"The war is over," he told her as they walked. "We are all going back to our civilian lives."

"What ship are you from?" Maryann pressed on.

"The Golden Griffin," he told her proudly.

"High Commander Tabbot's own flagship?" Maryann asked in shock and disbelief.

"Yes, but I really must go now," he asserted. She let loose his arm.

"But Sarsen Tabbot? What is she doing?" she called after him.

"She told us that her time had passed. She thanked us for our service. She didn't say exactly, but we all understood that she was retiring," he told her as he turned to walk away.

"Really?" Maryann asked just to be clear.

"Look around you. Isn't that obvious?" he told her in parting.

Maryann found her transport and quickly left for the meeting, half-way across town, that she knew was waiting for her. As she arrived, there was already a heated discussion in progress that quickly quieted when they saw her walk in.

"Well?" Malik asked her.

"You are not going to believe this; Sarsen Tabbot has disbanded her battle group."

"You have got to be kidding me," Malik said, stunned by this.

"She sent her people home. She thanked them for their service," Maryann went on.

"Good heavens! She called in the dogs and pissed on the fire," one of the men in the meeting exclaimed crudely.

"We are screwed," Malik said softly. "Get her on the com."

"She will not speak to you," the man in charge of communications told him minutes later.

"What did she say?" Malik asked, quickly approaching furious.

"Her Officer of the Watch told me that I could hold my hand on my ass waiting for her to call you."

"But she is our only defense!"

"I told him that. He said that was not at all true. He suggested that we call Union Fleet and see how long it takes them to get here, but he was laughing the whole time."

"Sarsen Tabbot cannot just retire!" Malik complained.

"That is exactly correct, but not what you think," a dark figure in the back of the room spoke up in a deep, gravelly voice. "She knows how much she is hated and feared. She will have to live out her days somewhere people do not know her."

"What are we going to do?" Malik addressed his council.

The dark figure spoke, "Sarsen Tabbot will leave the better part of her ships right here. I suggest that you start right away to recruit some crews and train them quickly. You will also need to find the shrewdest commander that you have left to lead them. And did I say that needs to be done right away?"

"Yes, you did," Malik replied. He looked at the others in the meeting. "Well, you heard the man. Start with the people Sarsen let go. Get some of them to stay on, even if it is only to train the new crews…"

<center>~~~</center>

Captain Chandrakar was coming to really dread whenever he received an incoming call from any of these Merc worlds beyond the Seven Pillars. Akheron was second only to Daggan-7.

"Yes, President Malik. How can we be of service to you today?" Captain Chandrakar asked with a pasted-on smile.

"We have a… situation here. It seems that Commander Tabbot has chosen this inopportune time to retire."

That one surprised Captain Chandrakar. "She retired, you say?"

"Yes, she did. That is why I am calling you," Malik told him.

"To give me this good news?"

"I would hardly call this good news!" Malik replied in controlled anger. "This is not good news at all. Without her battle group, the Seven Pillars planets are open to attack."

"Well, it sounds to me like you really need to replace her then," Captain Chandrakar advised him in all seriousness.

"Yes, we are in the process of doing just that, but that will take time. In that interim, we are calling upon the Union to provide us protection under the Treaty of Akheron."

Captain Chandrakar flinched when he heard that but recovered nicely. All of his well-laid plans to explore this region just went up in smoke one more time right before his very eyes!

"Union Fleet stands ready to live up to our side of the treaty," Ravi Chandrakar assured Malik.

Malik smiled. "Thank you, Captain Chandrakar. The people of the Seven Pillars Region thank you for your service." With that, he signed off.

Captain Ravi Chandrakar was beside himself angry. He grabbed something off his desk without even looking and threw it right through the now fading 3D display hologram. His swearing was interrupted only by the task-bot cleaning up the mess from the shattered java mug on the floor.

~~~

Across the Seven Pillars sector, Sarsen Tabbot saw the chaos she had created and smiled.
~~~

Chapter Seventeen
Intermezzo.

The Tesseract fleet landed on their own home field on Panara-5 at 04:23 Zulu. Everyone on board was asleep but John and Angel. Kip Landed in his usual place, as did all of the M-4s. It was a beautiful, crisp, clear night, a bit on the cool side. John put down the gangway and just sat there, enjoying the sweet smell of home.

John took out his tablet and called up his mother's Bible. "And I saw a new heaven and a new earth: for the first heaven and the first earth are passed away; and the sea is no more," he read out loud into the quiet of the night. He looked around at his home field with all of the ships. He looked up at the sky all full to overflowing with stars.

"Sure," he decided, "A new heaven and a new Earth. I suppose that could be. I only wish that my mother could have known that. It sure would have made her happy."

After the silence had once more closed in around him, his thoughts moved on.

"Hey Dad! They found it! It was right there all the time, just like you always said it was!" John told the wind. "I will go for a looksee myself someday." John took in a full dose of silence before he continued, "Sorry Mom, but you have to know better than anyone else that I am way too full of piss and vinegar to be any kind of a holy man." All of that settled, he was tired and headed for bed.

~

At 07:00, John got up. Much to his surprise, so did Mariah, and there was something seriously wrong here – she was cheerful. She even took a shower with him. On the wall-size, 3D display in the mess was the view out the forward camera of a glorious sunny day. A few wisps of clouds only added to the perfect picture of home.

"It was too chilly to set up breakfast outside," Jane told them as her android brought out his java and her tea.

"Jane, you know, I never did ask you what do you call your android," Mariah asked her.

"She is my sous-chef, so I just call her Sue. I think she is happy with that, too," Jane told her when Sue brought them out their breakfasts.

"Thank you, Sue," Mariah told her.

"You're welcome," Sue replied with a smile.

"You know," Jane confided in John and Mariah, "Sue loves to cook as much as I do. Isn't that just a kick in the seat -- an android that loves to cook? I never heard of such a thing, but I couldn't be happier." John knew full well why Sue loved to cook. It was the same 'why' that made Henry's android as ornery as Henry. It was the same 'why' as the artificial copilots all being as oversexed and free-spirited as Jessica. At that moment, he thanked his lucky stars that Mariah was never an android. One tough little butt-crack on this ship was as much as he would ever care to handle.

That was just ahead of the girls coming in, Sam arriving and Jim. Jessica and Henry were the last to arrive.

"Big day, Jim?" Henry asked him.

"Yeah. I have to go settle a few things and close down my apartment."

"Call me when you're ready. I will bring Andy and the LZ over to help you get your stuff," Henry offered.

"Thanks. I will do that," Jim kindly accepted.

Breakfast broke up with everyone going to see to their own agenda.

~

John worked on Barbie's ship himself once more. He was adding the slipstream drive components when Sophie and Emma came out to see him. They found him lying on his back with his head stuck into an open access port at the time, so they sat down with Barbie while he was busy.

"Emma needs to ask Dad something, and I came out to visit with you," Sophie told Barbie.

"That is very nice," Barbie told Sophie. "I love visitors." They all sat and had a nice chat while John finished what he was working on… without any swearing.

"You really should come over to the Tesseract and visit with us more often," Sophie told Barbie. "When you are not busy, of course."

"Yes, maybe I will do that," Barbie agreed.

John crawled out of the access port when he was finished. He brushed himself off and joined the chat group in progress in Barbie's mess.

"What did you want to ask me?" he asked Emma.

"What you are doing with these lasers," she asked him. "I totally understand how a starship works by adjusting its fields and generating a timequake, but I can't find anything about lasers and slipstream drives."

"That would be because no one else knows anything at all about it. This is all leading-edge science."

"Well?" she asked. After all, Emma's studies of timequake technology had already taken her to doctorate level studies. She was more highly qualified in this subject than he was.

"I really hadn't thought about it, but sure. Let's give it a go. Come on," he told Emma. "Let me set you up." They went back to John's office on the Tesseract. He called up the Codex files. It was somehow strange now, with Jessica's tattoo gone, that the Codex now simply recognized him. He rather missed picturing Jessica's naked backside in his mind.

This time, he commanded, [Security, Emma Korbin, access authorized.]

[Emma Korbin, access granted,] the Codex replied.

"Now Emma dear, these files are a family secret. No one else must ever see them but you."

Her whole face lit up.

"I love secrets," she told him.

"I know," he replied. "So do I."

"Where do I start?" she asked when she saw all of the alien pictographs.

"Just tell it, [Beginning]," he showed her. It opened up to the first study block for her.

Emma went right to her new study, thoroughly engrossed.

John and Sophie went back to Barbie's ship. John went back to work while Sophie and Barbie just sat and talked. John left the other ships' modifications to Henry, but he wanted to do the work on Barbie's ship himself. He told Henry that he needed to keep his head in the game, but Barbie knew that it was really because the Captain liked her best. She reveled in the warmth of being the Captain's favorite.

Jane was a big help to Barbie. She sent over food when she knew that The Captain would be hungry. *He sure likes to eat. It must be a bio thing,* Barbie thought. *Sophie seems to have his same appetite. Actually, Jessica is no slouch when it comes to eating either. And talk about eating; Henry eats even more than the Captain.* That seemed odd to Barbie, considering that the Captain was a very big man and Henry was just a wiry little guy. Even funnier was that Henry always wolfed his food down as if someone would steal it if he didn't.

<center>~~~</center>

Six skeleton freighters pulled into orbit around Kharon-3, taking adjacent orbital slots. Almost immediately, the tugs began arriving, loaded with spaceworthy containers. To watch the androids transfer the shipping containers from the tugs to the skeleton freighters, one would almost believe that a space ballet was being performed. It was so full of form and rhythmic motion that you could almost hear the "Dance of the Sugar Plum Fairy" playing faintly in the background.

What was really going on was the biggest heist in the history of mankind. Over many years, the Syndicate had taken its ill-gotten gains in diamonds, rubies, sapphires, and about every other form of precious gem as well as gold, silver, and platinum. Ten percent of the Syndicate's entire acquired wealth was socked away, accumulated against hard times, and hidden in the salt mines on Kharon-3 and Baratti-4.

Don't think for one minute that this secret was easily given up either, but Al Simmonds did hire some of the best data miners in the Union. It was just a small anomaly that cracked open the secret just a little bit. Unmarked shipping containers came in to Daggan-7 from all over the quadrant. Nikola's operation accumulated them and forwarded them on to Kharon-3 and Baratti-4. It was the only operation from which Nikola took no cut and was not paid for. In fact, the whole operation would have been invisible had it not been that Nikola had to fund the operation. His accounting people gave it an account with no name, only a number. Money only flowed in. That was the anomaly that caught their attention. Every other account showed a cash outflow to Nikola.

Even with an accounting trail, this secret would have still been secure had not a freighter pulled in with some 'special' shipping containers. All of the low-level people still did their jobs and forwarded the containers, just as they had always done. Then they charged their time to that special account, but now that account was frozen so the charge would not go through. Their new supervisor hadn't a clue as to what that was all about, so he called accounting.

From there, the hunt was on! One small ship followed the outbound freighter. Al Simmonds' new people on Kharon-3 and Baratti-4 were tasked to following the trail from there. The salt mines were quickly found, but over the many years, they had evolved into many thousands of kilometers of endless mazes and dead-end quantum portals. One quick-witted man put a dummy container into the system with a tracker, but the android vehicle took a winding path to deposit the container alone, in a dead-ended quantum portal.

The next answer came from the accounting department, when they estimated that the salt mines on both planets contained approximately 185,497 containers. At 15,600 containers per skeleton freighter, it would take twelve of the largest freighters that money could buy to move it all. But that would assume that they could find it.

It took Big Al's best Information Technology people to finally discover that a database existed right before their very eyes. The digitized map for the salt mines contained the encrypted data. The same android vehicles that stored the containers had software to access that encrypted data. All that need to be done was to tell the android vehicles to retrieve a specific container. But cracking this secret turned out to be the easy part.

An executive meeting was held to solve the hard part.

"We can't possibly store all of that loot here on Daggan-7," Frank concluded, "and we have no way to protect it even if we did."

"Disperse it all," came the quiet voice of Samuel Tczoroski.

"Say what?" Big Al asked for clarification.

"Make it impossible for anyone to get it all back. Disperse it all over as many of the Union planets as we can. Buy up businesses. Buy up property. Invest it all across the Union in so many places that it could never all be found and reclaimed. Best of all, the Union will be right there the whole time, protecting it for us."

"Sam, you are a genius," Al complimented him.

"That's why I get the big bucks," Sam quipped back with a smile.

"You sure will. You are in charge of doing exactly that, investing our newfound wealth. See me after the meeting. We will discuss your new salary," That put a smile on Sam's face.

~

Sam did indeed see Big Al privately after the meeting. Big Al saw to it that Sam would be handsomely rewarded. That was item one.

"Now I have another directive for you, but one that only you and I will ever discuss. Am I being perfectly clear?"

"Yes, sir," Sam answered, a bit puzzled.

"I want you to buy up every single business owned by Loretta Zharn, but here's the hitch; I want you to pay double what it is worth, triple if you can. I want you to make Loretta Zharn wealthy, and I do mean seriously wealthy. Am I clear on this point?"

"Yes, sir, Mister… President. I will do exactly that."

"Good. I want Zharn Interplanetary and all of its subsidiaries for myself. As for the rest: that we want to make the best investments that we can."

"I will hire the best investment specialists on each planet to make the purchases and watch over our investments for us," Sam agreed. "It will all be perfectly legitimate."

"But you will handle this private matter yourself," Al Simmonds directed him.

"I will handle this private matter myself, very discretely," Sam replied. He and Big Al shook on it. Sam left immediately for his new assignment.

Al Simmonds was once more alone in his office.

"Revenge is a dish best served up cold," Al Simmonds repeated the ages old cliché. "It may be as old as dirt, but it sure says exactly how I feel." Stealing the Syndicate's best-kept secret made him happier than a bird with a French-fry.

"I will make my Loretta and Ginger fabulously wealthy," he set in his mind. "I cannot be with them yet, but soon. If this all works out, then soon. My wife and daughter are the only ones I ever loved, the only ones who ever loved me."

The lie he told himself is that he did all of this for them, but we know better. They would have gladly lived as paupers to have him by their sides, but that was long ago. His daughter was just a baby when he had staged his own untimely demise by quantum bomb. She surely would not know his face, his voice, how much he loved her, but his Loretta would.

~~~

Sarsen Tabbot's voice now echoed in her flagship, the Golden Griffin. Since most of the crew had been dismissed on Akheron, it had become just a shell of the hustling, bustling hammer of war that it once was. The few people that remained on board were all loyal, trusted warriors, just like her. Long ago, they had given up family and friends, just as she had. Now, she was their everything. They had nothing to go back home for. They knew no other existence but this. They would follow her to the gates of hell.

For as huge a ship as was the Golden Griffin, it could dance with the best of them. It danced an intricate course through a space no one would ever have ever guessed it would fit. Two of the finest Merc pilots who ever flew a starship maneuvered it into the tiny cavern that would be its final resting place.

Almost in eerie silence, the shuttles left the Golden Griffin to its fate. A whole fleet of shuttles emerged from the huge cavern in an asteroid absolutely indistinguishable from all the other asteroids. The fleet of shuttles made their way to yet another asteroid… or so it appeared.
~~~

As they approached, a section of it opened. Inside the hollow 'asteroid' was a full space-dock with three brand new Phoenix-Class ships of war, slightly larger than a Union light cruiser but seriously more powerful. Phoenix-Class ships boasted three sets of engines to make them incredibly agile for a ship that big. Their shields were the best of the best, and their pulse-cannons were more powerful than even the Golden Griffin's.

The Phoenix-Class ships themselves were artificially intelligent, requiring minimal crews. The fleet of shuttles brought more than sufficient officers and crew to operate them. Three hours was all it took for the crews to stow their gear and take their new places.

"Loose the hounds of war," Sarsen commanded to release the ships from space dock and set them free. "Damn you all to hell," she cursed the people who would have reduced her to mere public servant. The ships all set course to a world known only to a select few and not on any charts, even her own. The coordinates all had to be input manually.

It was five days' journey even for as fast as these ships were. The whole five days, Sarsen hardly spoke. Her crew hardly spoke, and when they did, it was in hushed tones. Sarsen's ships arrived at their destination and entered orbit not only unchallenged but also without so much as a single word.

A single shuttle brought Sarsen to the surface of a world whose beauty was second to none. The Earthlike world had three moons to stabilize its rotation and no tilt to its axis. Thus, its weather was always mild, with just a whisper of some high cirrus clouds in a deep azure sky. The shuttle approached a city that appeared to flow along with the natural shapes of the land that it was built on. Her shuttle landed on a pad of fine hand-set stone.

When the shuttle door opened, Sarsen exited, but no one was there. Her security squad quickly formed up to escort her to where the only path led to a portal on a huge marble wall. On the far side of the portal was a private courtyard. As they entered, they found a tall, well-built man in white flowing robes. His light brown hair and beard were immaculately trimmed, accenting the perfect skin of his very masculine face.

"I was expecting you," was all he said in a deep resonant voice as she approached.

By her signal, the security squad held back as she continued on.

"What else was I to do? Where else to go?"

"So finally, we meet face-to-face, but you look as if this is some kind of end."

"Haven't you heard? The war was lost," she answered. After all, this was old news.

"Of course, we heard, dear Sarsen, but we beg to differ. The war was not lost. Neither was it won," he told her in soothing tones, as though to console her.

"But there was a surrender to Union forces at Zari-Kuut," Sarsen argued, still bewildered by his line of reasoning.

"Yes, so sad. Even so, Union forces did not secure their victory, so it was all for naught."

"But Merc forces were defeated," Sarsen reminded him.

"So, it would appear," he answered with a smile.

"So, it would appear?" she questioned his answer.

"My dear Sarsen, there is a very old Earth saying 'It ain't over till the fat lady sings.' Well, the fat lady hasn't sung yet," he told her.

Chapter Eighteen
Entangled by fate.

John, Henry, and Kip took the entire fighter wing into space for trial runs with the new slipstream drives. Each ship had already been meticulously checked and tested. This was more of a tactical shakedown cruise for training the copilots.

"Let's start with a locked field formation," John began. "In a locked field configuration, only the lead ship turns on its lasers. For this exercise, I will be the lead ship."

The copilots all locked fields. Then John lit up Barbie's lasers.

"Notice that we still have quantum-com," John told them, "but my lasers generate so many timequakes that they spread our existence over time. To anyone in normal space, we just disappeared."

"But I can look out my starboard camera and see you," Kip replied.

"That is only because we are jumping all over near time together. You will see next that when we all turn on our own lasers, we will not be able to see each other."

"But will our quantum-coms still work?" Kip asked.

"We are about to find that out," John told him, "but first, I want each pilot to try this locked field slipstream drive for themselves." Over the next few hours, they did exactly that.

"Remember that locked field mode works for any number of ships," John told them all. "If one ship lost its lasers, another ship could lock fields to get them both into slipstream."

Next, they tried slipstream, each ship on its own. The exercise was simple: just go to the next waypoint, but the effects were far more complicated.

"Does the quantum-com still work?" John inquired over the network.

"Yes, thankfully," Kip came back. "I felt like I was suddenly all alone."

"Yes," Lisa responded. The other copilots were quick to return to their normal network chatter now that they knew it worked.

"While we all have this peaceful time together, I am promoting all of my lady copilots. You have all earned the full rank of pilot. I am very proud of each one of you."

That made four ladies very happy. Kip and Rachel had already worked out their very complex relationship long ago.

When the happy talk returned to the here and now, Ciara asked, "In separate mode, how do we know where the other ships are?"

"Quantum-com," John answered her. "We will have to work that out. Also, please note that to a ship with slipstream drive, waypoints are meaningless. That will take some getting used to. All of your weapons systems are just as meaningless. In order to use them, you will have to drop out of slipstream just long enough to fire, then go back into slipstream drive to disappear."

At the end of a long, exhausting two days, John and Kip were happy with the results of this shakedown cruise. They were ready for some R & R. Henry was mostly along to monitor all of the new equipment, but he was always ready for some R & R.

~

Where else but the Pig and Whistle would you take some R & R? It was supposed to be just a cozy, relaxing night out for the Tesseract family, but as you already know, the road to hell is paved with good intentions. When John first mentioned that he would like to have a nice family night at the Pig and Whistle, Mariah knew, of course, that included Kip and Rachel, but she kind of missed Kira and Gina too, so she invited Ishmael and family. She also missed her Luke, so she invited Luke, Rebecca, and their whole family.

It got even bigger when one of the local veterans found out from the waitress at the Pig and Whistle that the Tesseract group would be gathering that night. That whole group of veterans congregated on the bar side, not being family.

It was between Mariah and Jessica who could take the longest to get ready for anything and make them late. John hated being late for anything. It made him crazy to know he was going to be late. John's tactic for dealing with this was to tell them that the reservation was for a half-hour earlier than it really was. Then they would leave the Tesseract about the same time they were supposed to be arriving at the Pig and Whistle. They would thus arrive on time, making John happy.

The family side of the Pig and Whistle was already full to overflowing when they walked in.

"I thought this was going to be a small family get-together," he said to Mariah in disbelief.

"You can't have a small family get-together when you have a big family," she came right back. "Who was I supposed to leave out?"

"The other half of the population of Panara-5," he came back, laughing at her.

She shook her fist at him. "Pow! Zoom!" she threatened.

He only laughed all the more. She smiled.

As these things tend to go, after the meal, the family groups tend to break up with the men congregating into a group and the ladies into their own group, but that drove Mariah nuts. It forced her to follow two conversations at the same time: the ladies' conversation and the men's.

Doctor Jim told the tale of his first voyage aboard the Tesseract, but he had to repeat himself constantly to Mariah when she couldn't hear every word of it. When he got to the part about the pirates, the subject of Earth came up.

"You can well imagine how surprised I was to find that the database you gave me," John told Ishmael privately, "already had the location of Earth."

"In Merc circles, that is a closely guarded secret that my ancestors and I have kept alive lo these many years. That data could have cost us our very lives. But that was then, and this is now. I am happy that Micah once found Earth too. And now you know too. Someday, maybe everyone will know."

John got up later to walk around and stretch his legs. He took a second to stand outside the open door and enjoy the quickly cooling night air. He looked up at the night sky. For that moment, his mind was at peace. Right here, right now, this is where he belonged. He took a long, deep breath of that.

"Many are called, but few are chosen," came the words from a stranger cloaked in darkness. "You were indeed chosen and set on the path."

"I chose my own path," John replied. He had been down this logical path before with Micah but wanted to see where the stranger would go with it.

"Free will and fate are equal, like energy and matter," the stranger put her argument into terms just for John. "On the quantum level, they are one and the same."

"I have never heard it put quite that way, but yes. On the quantum level, they are one and the same," John agreed, referring to the quantum nature of energy and matter.

"Humanity is quantum in nature, too," the stranger continued. "Each human being is but a single quantum of Humanity. And, just like quantum entanglement in physics, human fates are all entangled. The smallest upset to the least of us sends ripples through all of quantum humanity to all the rest of us. We are entangled by fate," the stranger made her argument in powerful tones. "When you first stepped foot upon the decks of your ship, that changed everything. The moment you first met each of the people that you now hold most dear, that changed everything." Now she had John's full attention. "It changed the future for each of you. It changed everything. You just have to be wise enough to see that."

"That is true," John had to admit after some thought.

"You became intimately entangled in their fates and them in yours. So, by fate were you put on this path, and you became forever entangled," the stranger closed her argument.

John felt a tug at his sleeve. He turned to find Emma.

"I just wanted to tell you; those files that you gave me set my mind on fire," she told him.

"They did the same to me," John agreed with a big smile.

She gave him a hug and a kiss on the cheek. "Thank you, Father. I love you."

"I love you too much to even say with words," he hugged her back.

"In that horrible shipping crate, I was alone and abandoned without hope, but then you found me," she said, looking him square in the eyes. "Somehow, in all of this huge universe, you found me, and that changed everything."

"My dearest Emma, I had lost everything that I held most dear in my heart, but then somehow, in all of this huge universe, I found you, and that changed everything," he told her.

"Who were you talking to?" Emma asked him, but when John turned back around, the stranger was gone. Seconds later, the stranger's voice echoed down the street from somewhere in the distance. She only said one word, "Entangled."